In A Family Way

Stories by Zeke Jarvis

Fomite

Burlington, VT

ISBN-13: 978-1-937677-99-2
Library of Congress Control Number: 2015933332

Fomite
58 Peru Street
Burlington, VT 05401
www.fomitepress.com

Cover image —
Author photo —

For my mother and father

Acknowledgements

Thank you to my family, my mother and father, my brother and his family, my wife and Angi, Nikki, Tina and Marcus. Thank you also to my wonderful colleagues, Jessica Barr, William Wright, Kathy Whitson, Jami and Scott Hemmenway, Junius Rodriguez, Erika Quinn, Mike Toliver, Prabhu Venkataraman, Mike Thurwanger and Amanda Frioli. Thanks to my closest friends in the writing world, Stephen Powers and Teresa Milbrodt. Thanks, too, to my teachers, Jim Hazard, Maurice Kilwein-Guevara, John McNally, Liam Callanan, Kim Blaeser and George Clark. Thank you to Marc Estrin and Donna Bister for their patience, guidance and support. Finally, thank you to the magazines that originally published versions of these stories. "Breaking Point" in *Falling Star Magazine*, "Expect Major Delays" in *Indigo Rising*, "Caillou" and "Supposedly Impervious to Fire" in *Petrichor Machine*, "Mr. Potatohead" in *Print Oriented Bastards*, "Eulogy" in *Kestrel*, "Disposal" in *Sobotka Literary Magazine*, "Toast" in *Heliotrope*, "Displays" in *Gravel*, "Bigfoot" in *SnReview*, "No Running" in *Work Literary Magazine*, "A Truly Awful Presence" in *Superstition Review*, "Feeling Not So Hot" in *Infinite Acacia*, "Part of Our House" in *Meat for Tea*, "Convergence" in *Scout and Engineer*, "The Posted Limit" in *2 Bridges Review*, "You're a Mother* in *Kestrel*, "The Kid Next Door" in *Rappahonock Review*, and "Man in a Windstorm" in *Rolling Thunder*.

Contents

Breaking Point

efore I really get into it, I'll just say that I've had my share of strange jobs. Not just weird ones that you've heard of like singing telegrams, baby namer or strip-club janitor, but some really out-there stuff like professional mourner or closed captions writer for porn DVDs (quick note: all the stuff that you'd think would be called "moans" should actually be "turn-on groaning" or "horny sounds" if the porn is low-budget enough, which it too often is). Forget all that. The job I'm about to describe wasn't the weirdest, but it had the craziest single work experience I've ever. My title, at the time was "rental scapegoat", which is exactly what it sounds like. People with stressful lives and/or anger issues would hire me to fuck with them in their homes just so that they could unload on me, but they'd feel justified, because I was fucking with them. It's what they wanted.

Mostly, people would only yell at me, but now and then they'd physically assault me a little. I mean, "assault" probably isn't a fair term. It's shit that was forbidden by the contract (I went through an agency that I found online, and they were surprisingly together), but I'd usually take a slap or a punch on the arm. Once, a guy punched me in the face, but he gave me a huge tip to balance that out, and it was actually really good advertising for me. In fact, I had a couple of black-eye pictures taken for my business cards. But that wasn't the big experience. It wasn't even out of the ordinary for the other agency guys. One of my colleagues once had his jaw broken. Instead of suing, he took a little cash from the assailant and spent the next couple of months developing his non-verbal aggression. After that, he made everyone's time at the agency hell, though nobody was really surprised. It fit his character.

That really was the problem with the job: you get used to being a prick. If you let up at all while you're on the clock, it breaks the fourth wall, and it's a hard thing to turn off. If the client's fat, you have to call them fat. If their spouse just died, then you have to make fun of them for crying. You have to observe people's most obvious weaknesses, and that's how you start to view the world. So there was this one client who'd just gone through a bitter divorce, and he needed an outlet for his rage. So, I come into his house, and, to start with, he's kind of timid, so I figure that I'll go ahead and be aggressive, to make him comfortable. So I'm going through pictures from his married life. I'm tossing them all over the floor and telling him "God, no wonder why your wife wanted to get out. Kid, too, probably". He'll say stuff like, "Oh," and "hey", but no major reaction, so I keep going. Finally, I see this little ashtray that was clearly made by some kid in a middle school art class. There's a black shelving unit with some electronics a couple decent pieces of art, and then this little nugget. It's green and kind of lumpy and has "Daddy" written in blue letters. I see it, then I look, and I see he sees me looking. The obvious thing here is to make fun of its crappiness. And it is crappy. But, well, that's obvious. So, I'm looking at it, and I'm trying to decide if I should break it, and I think he sees that. Here's the problem again: If I don't smash it, crappy as it is, then he knows I have limits and he feels safe. Maybe he can't unload, because he knows. If I break it, then I can't undo what I've done, so if I have crossed a line, I can't really apologize.

The ashtray is on a shelf, so I decide I'll start pushing it off, very slowly, looking at the client and smiling the whole time. And it's getting to the edge, and he says, "No." And now I smile even wider and push it just a bit further. His voice is really quiet, and he says, "Don't be an asshole." But I'm not totally sure if he means it, and it's not a thing you can ask. So I give it one last push, and it falls off the edge. But either the shelf wasn't high enough or, somehow, this little turd of an ashtray was quality made, because it doesn't break. So the client and I are staring at it, and he says, "Thank God."

But I could've sworn that he kind of sighed, too, so I think I'll try one last time. I pull my foot back and I kick as hard as I can. Sure enough, this time it hits the wall, bounces and then cracks into three pieces. They all go off in slightly different directions, and I wonder if he sees that as a metaphor or a cliché. Either way, he starts screaming. Really screaming at me. Cursing, threatening my family, that kind of shit. Though even that's kind of normal. Spit's flying, and I can feel the heat off his face. All this shit is kind of standard too, but today I feel like I actually deserve it. Even in my job. I actually felt like a prick in that moment.

Eventually, though, he goes to his desk, and he pulls out a revolver, and I just freeze. He comes to me and says, "Open your mouth" in a flat tone. And I do, though I'm thinking I should just run. The agency didn't prepare me for this. I don't feel comfortable saying this is part of the act, but I'm not totally sure it's not either. And that's when I wonder if this is how my clients feel while I'm fucking with them.

So he puts the gun in my mouth, and I'm surprised by how heavy the barrel feels on my teeth, and I already feel my drool starting to come, and he says, "You fucking prick," and he just stares, and I don't know if I should cry or beg or what. And I don't know, because I'm not even sure if my life is at stake or not. And if I break the fourth wall, will that only piss him off even more? Then the guy leans in even closer, his nose touching my cheek, and his lips start to blow back and forth. His spit is just covering my cheek. Then, when I'm sure he's going to kill me, he breaks down and starts sobbing. He's sobbing, but he leaves the gun in my mouth, and I don't move. When the gun comes out of my mouth, it clanks against my teeth a little, and the guy slides to the floor. He crumples. I pat him on the back, and he hugs me, but I still feel the gun in his hand. It's kind of pressing into the back of my head, but the side and not the barrel. And I feel okay, now.

Once he collects himself, he asks me if I could come back, maybe break something else. I thank him for his interest, but I tell him it wouldn't be the same thing again. "Lightning in a bottle" I say, though I'm not sure if that's the right phrase. He nods, either way. As I leave, he shakes my hand, and he tips me really fucking big. And I never see him or hear from him again, and it's shortly after that when I start looking for a new line of work. I might have been on my way out anyway, what with the broken-jaw guy and all, but this was definitely the one thing that pushed me out the door. And that was fine.

Before the announcment, Clay always felt guilty watching Claire cut celery. She was the expert, giving even and thin strips, but it seemed unfair that her care and skill made her do all the work. Now, since they'd confirmed that the world was ending, he felt puzzlement more than guilt. In fact, he kind of hated watching her cook now.

"All that fucking science," Claire said, rinsing another stalk. "They know how and what day it's going to happen, and they can't do Jack shit about it. Not Jack-fucking shit."

Claire hadn't sworn much before the coming apocalypse became public knowledge, but since the scientific community set the date as April 14th of next year, the floodgates had opened. Clay was disappointed; he'd thought that swearing would be his thing. "Fuck," he said, but without much pleasure.

"What, Honey?" Claire asked.

"Nothing." He walked over to the counter where Claire was cutting the vegetables and took a matchstick-piece of carrot. "Why don't we get delivery?" He laid the stick in his mouth and munched.

Claire waved her hand. "Everyone orders out now. Besides, I like to cook."

Clay nodded. "Thought any more about the orgies?"

Claire stopped chopping, but didn't look at him. "Not today, Clay."

He cleared his throat, and she started chopping again. The celery looked wilty. Produce had gone to shit. But it would be fine once it hit the heat and oil of the pan. At least there was that.

***

At first, Clay was appalled by the orgies. They were a knee-jerk and disgusting response, exactly the kind of thing that the wicked would do as Judgment Day approached. But, as the day drew nearer, the thought of being part of one big ball of carnal flesh, of really experiencing the physical world before having to leave it, that sounded all right to Clay. And in all the footage that he'd seen the orgies never seemed violent. No rape or shoving, just a bunch of people having sex out in the open.

In his monitoring, Clay was surprised by how even-handed the press had turned out to be. After the orgies had gone into public places, The Today Show had had on a cop, a priest, and an orgy participant talking about them. Katie Couric had moderated their discussion. She'd had her hair the way Clay really liked it. That sort of sweep that almost covered her cheek. Katie started the discussion off by talking with the orgy participant.

The participant and the priest were arguing, pretty much what Clay had expected, but the cop had said something interesting. Katie asked, "Chief Paulson, people are saying that the police are already turning a blind eye to the orgies. Is this true, and, if it is, then what's the thinking behind allowing this to go on?"

"Well, Katie," the cop said, "we have had to reprioritize significantly since the announcement. Between the violent and extensive rioting and the members of the force who've decided to just stay at home with their families, which I'm not putting down, but it's a reality we're being forced to address…with all that, we've been stretched extremely thin as it is. These problems, plus the fact that we really haven't received many official complaints about the orgies have led them to not being a primary area of concern for us relative to the more immediate crimes being committed."

Katie stopped the nodding she'd been doing as the chief spoke. "I see. And what about those who say that this reprioritizing basically works out to a tacit endorsement of the orgies?"

The Chief shifted a little. "I guess I'd just say to anyone making that particular criticism: 'Look, I think you'd rather have us protecting your homes from being shot at or burned to the ground than having us send out our people to break up orgies that are just going to start back up a couple hours after they're dispersed.' Do you know how many man hours it would take to process all the arrested participants from an orgy? It'd be ridiculous. And, Katie, I'm not going to post officers at sites just to keep orgies from starting up again. Not unless we're getting official reports of rape, child molestation, or bestiality."

The priest started to argue, the participant butted in, and Katie wrapped up the segment, thanking all three guests, but pointing out time constraints. They switched over to a piece on how suicide rates were increasing, which Clay thought was weird.

***

Clay had been promoted just a month or so before the announcement. He'd planned on waiting to see if the position worked out; he and Claire might've been ready for a move. If they were going to move, then they'd have to do it before he got too far up the ladder to get out. After the announcement, though, a lot of the workers he was supposed to be supervising had stopped showing up. And a lot of those that did show up didn't bother to respect him any more. Even a couple that he'd been fairly close to, personally. Luckily, his high-up superiors didn't come in either. He'd tried adopting the government's new slogan: "Let's all pitch in," but the workers all told him that the slogan was created for the utilities workers, not office drones. Clay tried pointing out that they still got a lot of phone calls from anxious customers, but even he didn't totally buy it.

One of his friends, Jackson, had become such a problem that he needed to be fired. Jackson had been asking all the women to join him at the orgies during the work day. The office couldn't afford to have him chasing off the few workers that did show up.

Clay called Jackson into his office. When Jackson came, Clay held out a hand to the chair across his desk. Jackson hesitated for a second, maybe wanting a handshake or something, and then he sat down.

"Jackson," said Clay, "I know it's a crazy and stressful time, but it's that way for everyone here, you know?"

"Angela had mentioned the orgies in the break room," said Jackson. "She has no right to complain about me."

Clay waved his hands and grimaced. "I'm not calling you in here to argue what Angela did or didn't say. It really doesn't matter, anyway, it's..."

"I know," said Jackson. "I know." He looked down at his pants and shook his head. His voice cracked when he started talking again. "It's just that, you're married and stuff. You'll be actually holding someone during the very last moment on Earth. You know?"

"Hey," said Clay folding his hands and leaning forward. He frowned for a second, then opened his top desk drawer and pulled out one of his bottles of booze, trying not to let them clink loudly enough for Jackson to know there were a few of them. Two scotch and one vodka. "Here," he said, breaking the seal on the cheaper bottle of scotch and passing it to Jackson. "Here you go."

Jackson nodded, sniffled, and took a slug from the bottle.

"Good, huh?" asked Clay.

"Clay…" Jackson wiped his nose and took a breath. "Do I get some kind of severance package? I mean, company policy—"

Clay opened his mouth and half shook his head. The men's mouths took turns opening and closing without making any real words, and then they began to laugh. They bent and shook and laughed a bit. Wiping his eyes, Clay said, "I'll make sure your pink slip goes to the office with the most absences. It won't get processed till…it won't get processed. And if I hold it on my desk a few days, what are they going to do? Fire me?"

The men began to laugh again, though not very hard this time.

***

Right up until the moment he and Claire got into their car, Clay thought that he'd be able to make a deal with her. He wouldn't complain about going to see her family, and then they'd stop at an orgy on the way home. But Claire had started in again about Clay making a point to see and hug his family instead of settling for a phone call, and Clay lost his heart. Claire only had one brother, some financial whiz, and her brother and her parents both lived less than an hour away. Clay had four siblings spread out over America, parents three states away, and a grandmother in a retirement home that was probably unstaffed right now. Clay'd called them all (except the grandmother), and said his goodbyes already. He was all right with that, and so were they.

As Claire was saying that her brother might be able to finagle them a helicopter ride to get to his parents' place, Clay cut in. "You'd better watch your swearing tonight. Your family will be surprised."

Clay kept his eyes on the road, but he could see Claire pull back and twist to look at his face. "Why do you hate my family?" she asked.

Clay swallowed, wishing that he could drain the heat out of the car. "Just please don't make me see my family. We talked to each other already. Besides, they know my work keeps me busy."

Claire turned back towards the windshield. "All right. Never mind, then."

"And I don't hate your family." Claire patted his leg. Clay sighed. "Is your mom making any red potatoes?"

"Yep. I told her to go ahead and leave a little skin on." Claire patted his thigh again, leaving her hand there a little longer this time. "I know you like them that way."

"It's sort of nice," said Clay. "Not having to worry about our weight or what food might clog our arteries. We can just let go."

Claire dropped her fists on her knees. "Clay," she said.

Clay glanced over at her and then looked back to the road. Since the apocalypse, freeways were clogged, and Clay wasn't as sure of himself on these back roads. They were a little busier, because of the freeways, but the real problem was the deer. Clay actually liked the reassurance of a few extra cars on the back roads. All the government had done for the freeways was to put up those digital signs that read, "Expect Major Delays".

Even with the deer, though, Clay wanted to look at Claire so he could prepare himself. She looked tired. Baggy eyes and slack lips. "What, Sweetie?"

"Is this about the orgies again?"

Clay coughed. "I wasn't specifically talking about that. I just meant that it's sort of nice that we'll be done with all our worries soon. We can relax now and just be together. Just be."

Claire nodded. "Yeah," she said, "I guess so."

***

After about three bites of his mother-in-law's salad, Clay already wanted a drink. Claire's brother was telling them about how a lot of activism was shifting from larger projects like legislation and organized demonstrations into more immediate concerns. "It's great; people wanted direction, and it just took a few phone calls and example favors to get the ball rolling. All those people who would otherwise be neglected get meals, companionship, shelter…"

Clay rubbed his eyes with the heels of his hands. His grandmother would've been 89 on April 20th of next year if there'd have been an April 20th next year.

"Something the matter, Clay?" asked Claire's mom.

Clay set his hands on his lap, opened his eyes, and said, "It's just a lot to take in, you know? End of the world."

Claire's brother nodded and puffed out his upper lip. "Sure is. But we all have to do what we can while we can."

"At least the rioters haven't gotten too far beyond the run-down parts of the cities." Claire quickly stuffed a forkful of lettuce into her mouth, her safeguard against having to produce a quick follow up.

Claire's mom set down her fork. "Isn't it just awful what the rioters did to the peaceful choirs?"

Clay shifted in his seat. The peaceful choirs had been a group of singers from every faith, signing hymns or chanting according to their beliefs. They wanted to bring peace to this world newly filled with uncertainty, but the first time they came up against the rioters, they got horribly, brutally murdered in the streets. The clip that had come to sum up that confrontation was a man in a backwards baseball cap standing on top of a truck and picking off singers with a shotgun. Clay remembered Matt Lauer apologizing for the graphic nature of the clip before airing it. Matt and Katie were wearing ribbons to commemorate the awful tragedy.

"At least we're safe here, Mom," said Claire's brother, offering a little smile.

"There's no place I'd rather be," said Claire's mom, and then the three of them began to cry. Clay set down his fork and chewed on his lip until it was over.

***

For all the weeping and uncomfortable moments that had gone on over the weekend with Claire's family, the car ride home seemed relatively chipper. Claire had thanked him twice for coming up there with her, she didn't mention his family at all, and she even said "I think you're right about skipping out on those Church services from now on. They've gotten too god-damned long and sappy." And she'd done it all in the first 20 minutes of the drive. After a couple minutes of happy silence, she said, "I suppose now you'll want me to return the favor by going to an orgy."

Clay frowned. "It's not that I need anyone else, you know." Claire kept quiet. "I just don't want any regrets," Clay said.

"Neither do I," said Claire. "And I think I'll regret fucking a bunch of strangers so close to when we go."

"If you don't want to, then we don't have to."

"So you'll just resent me for our last few months on Earth?"

Clay shook his head. He wanted to admit that he didn't like Claire's family, but that would get neither of them anywhere. As the two of them fidgeted, a deer broke out of the woods across the road. Clay slammed on the breaks and they both jerked forward then back. They'd stopped well short of the deer, but Clay was still shaking. He and Claire looked over at each other. They laughed and then kissed. The rest of the ride home was quiet, but things were different.

***

Clay shook for just a second as he and Claire got close to the actual sex on a field of grass. They'd made their way through the crowds that were just standing and watching. Claire's post-deer flip on the orgies had happened so quickly that Clay hadn't had time to think about what exactly he'd do when they got there. He realized that if he added up all of the people that he'd actually seen naked in his life, it would be less than the group of people he saw naked now, in front of him.

13

Claire kept her eyes on the orgy and asked, "So I guess we're supposed to disrobe now?"

Clay looked at her. Her hair was up, which she never did for sex with him. He loved when her hair would drag over his chest or his belly during sex. He looked back at the orgy and was a little intimidated by the fact that there were more toned and tanned bodies than what he'd expected. "Well," said Clay, "if we take our clothes off, then that's about it. We have to go in."

Claire smiled at Clay, although her eyes didn't look into it. "Having second thoughts?"

Clay chuckled. "Second and third, I guess."

She touched his arm. "Sweetie, it's just the world, just our bodies. It really doesn't matter if we do this or not."

"Uh-huh," said Clay. He did a quick scan and was grateful to see there were no television cameras around. One guy looked over towards them, then held out his hand and waved for them to come in. He kept thrusting while he did it, so his wave was jerky. Clay shivered. "Let's go home."

Claire raised one eyebrow, shrugged, and turned. As she took a few steps away from the sex, some of the crowd watching the orgy booed. Claire looked back at Clay, who hadn't taken a step in either direction. The boos and chanting made any kind of intimate communication impossible. Claire yelled, "Go ahead. I'll still be here when you're done."

Clay looked around. "You're not coming?"

Claire just shook her head, keeping her smile.

Clay looked at the ground. "It wouldn't feel like cheating if you'd come in with me."

"What?" yelled Claire.

"Nothing." Clay shook his head.

"Clay," said Claire, "Just go and be happy. It's okay. It really is okay with me."

Clay looked at his wife. Her eyes had sort of warmed into her smile. He smiled back and blew her a kiss. She caught it and put it on her cheek, and then she patted it onto her ass, like she used to do when they'd first started dating. They both laughed. Clay turned and tugged at his robe's belt. The crowd opened up and cheered so he could make his way in. His hands were shaking as he slid his robe all the way off.

Caillou

My possible future stepkid is sitting on the couch with me. I'm sort of grading papers, and she's very much watching Caillou, which is this goofball cartoon. What I mean by goofball is that the family doesn't yell at each other; they solve problems rationally. And they're Canadian, so everybody is polite and helpful. I can understand why this appeals to Emma, but I only get sucked in by a kind of cynical interest. This episode has a child with what I assume to be Down syndrome visiting the daycare, which I guess they call "playschool" in Canada, that Caillou attends with his friends. It took me a while to figure out that the kid had Down syndrome. It wasn't until he couldn't figure out how to use the swing. The animators tried to signal the disease with some lines around the eyes. Caillou is a cartoon with very few lines, so it made the kid look like he had huge bags under his eyes, like he had some horrible life and couldn't sleep or relax. Like Tweak from Southpark. I didn't get Down syndrome from that at all.

I look down at Emma. I wonder what she thinks is happening this episode. At three (and a half), I don't know that she's ever seen someone with a mental disability. I offer her some apple juice, and she takes it without looking at me. I start to feel bad for not inter-acting with her more. But it's hard. I've been around her for a year and a half, and I'm not really familiar with kids. Now the kids on Caillou are playing a pretend game, where the Down kid is pre-tending to be a dragon. I look down at a student paper about how Hamlet is for sure actually crazy, and I wonder what it's like to be a voice actor pretending to be a kid with Down syndrome pretending to be a dragon. What does the director say to you?

Whether I stay in her life or not, I want Emma to have a good life. Even if she can be a shit sometimes. Maybe I just feel this way because I'm sitting next to her on the couch and she's quiet and serene. Right now, her mother is at work, and I'm technically on Spring break.

***

Emma and I will often roleplay. She'll look at me and call me Emma, then she'll ask, "Why didn't you eat your vegetables, Emma?" I'll say something like, "I don't like beans. I wanted carrots." This will go back and forth until she inevitably puts me in time out for throwing a pretend tantrum. Or for pretending to throw a tantrum, maybe. There's a difference, of course, even in Emma's mind. Today, I'm sitting next to a Caillou figure missing its thumb and an empty juice box. Some combination of us are responsible for Emma (who, for the purposes of time out, is me) getting a juice spill on the papers s/he is grading. "Don't talk in time out," she says. I actually don't mind sitting in time out, because I can sketch out a lesson plan or get a concept or two articulated on my dissertation. But, today, my pen ran out of ink, and as I mutter something to

17

Caillou, I get reprimanded. I shake my finger at the juice box and say, "It was her."

Emma stops and looks back at me. "It's a boy." In all fairness, the drink box is blue, and it has a picture of what could be a male apple riding on a skateboard. I wonder if anyone designing the box read the Bible much. "It was him." Emma starts laughing at me. "You're silly."

It strikes me that this is how a lot of my dating life has gone, too. In fact, it's how I met Emma's mother. My evermore-serious girlfriend. When we first met, I assumed that she was married, so I felt comfortable flirting with her. Not that I look to cuckold other guys (I enjoy using the verb cuckold more than thinking about helping to create the noun). I'm more confident talking to women if there's no possibility of things coming to fruition. We pretended to flirt, then really flirted, then things went from there while I was still registering that I was actually flirting. .

"You drink the juice," Emma says. It's not a suggestion.

"I drink coffee," I say. "You're silly."

"Coffee smells bad."

I nod. A lot of the shows I watched as a kid were based on antagonism. Ernie fucking with Burt. Bugs Bunny harassing Elmer Fudd. It's hard for me to communicate through Emma's earnestness. She gets angry with me sometimes, because I don't know how to respond. I sometimes feel that way with the students I teach in comp, too. With Emma's mother, I think she assumes I'm sympathetic, because I like to be quiet and nod. Or I like to think she thinks I'm sympathetic. Maybe she just feels motherly by taking in this awkward child.

***

My grad school friends and I like to have regression nights. Usually around the midterm exam period. Regression means that we act stupid, immature. That we balance out all of our intellectual exploration with dumb acts of physicality. My closest friend would give a long explanation of how this was in keeping with Native cosmologies involving tricksters, who have a foot in both the world of the divine and the profane world of man. When he was done, he'd fart as long and loud as he could. Interestingly, he never seemed to have a problem farting at length. His dissertation involved looking at recent rereadings of Foucault and Nietzsche juxtaposed with oral narratives from Vaudeville performers. The title was *Throwing Tomatoes from the Panopticon*. To be honest, I'd never read a single word of it.

One regression night, our chosen act of idiocy was to do headstand insobriety tests. No one was allowed to stumble home if they could sustain upside-down verticality. Somebody came up with it while watching someone do a keg stand at an earlier party. So this regression night, one of our fellow partygoers had done his third shot of tequila, all with beer chasers, and he ended up swinging down and crashing into a huge ceramic hand in the goat-throwing position. My best friend got it from a former girlfriend. An art major who was in one of this comp classes. The hand, of course, cracked. My best friend shrugged it off. The other guy apologized, but then went to get a drink. After he left the room, my best friend unzipped his fly, slid one of the broken fingers into it, and let it dangle. "He can suck it," he said.

Nobody laughed. I went to get another drink, too. That night, I faked falling over so I could go home early. He never said anything, but I always assumed my best friend could tell.

***

There's this other show, Superwhy, where reading makes this kid, Wyatt (the title character's alter ego), a superhero. It's a very interesting concept in that power is linked to the ability to read, to make sense of stories and draw morals that directly apply to a "real-life" problem. I tried to get Emma to watch it, but she wouldn't sit still for it. She hated it. I wanted her to like it, but I also felt like too much of an asshole making her watch something because it fit my egghead agenda. I feel that way every day with my comp classes. I don't know how to feel about interesting them in academia.

I don't like to say what my dissertation's about, either. Not just to my comp classes, but to anyone. It has to do with discourse analysis and sketch comedy. There's some joke that's about grad school teaching you how to hate the things you used to enjoy. I still like Kids in the Hall, some of the State, and, well, I actually even hate Monty Python these days. I don't know how people read Shakespeare anymore. I don't know how people read or watch anything, to be honest. In the past 5 years, I've gotten really good at complaining. What's even more idiotic is that I actually spend time thinking about what my specific complaints, and the formulation of said complaints, "mean". This is how I spend my time. Emma likes to watch television and color and see what inedible objects she can bite or lick.

In order to be a good little grad student, to be someone who's going to get a tenure-track job, I'm the grad student rep on the WAC committee. I generally don't speak, which, I think, is what is expected from me. Not speaking, I mean. But there was one time, when someone mentioned students proving a thesis. One of the folks from the hard sciences interrupted my colleague to say that, in his discipline, you don't prove a thesis; you test it, because a thesis is up for grabs. At the time, this seemed like a really important point to me, so I started saying that, by "prove", we in the humanities often mean that you support your claims, but leave it open. Papers are arguments, invitations for debates. I was explaining this, and I realized, from the looks around the table, that people were watching the clock and not listening to me, so I trailed off after asserting the importance of standardization in grading criteria.

In addition to Caillou, my possible future stepdaughter also enjoys a show called Handy Manny. In it, there's tools that talk and move and act out silly antics. In one episode, they were playing with a top, and it went around and hit each tool. There are eight tools total, and by the time the last two (Turner, a flathead screwdriver, and Squeeze, a pliers, if it matters) got hit, they were just standing there, having to know what would happen. I looked over at Emma and wondered about these shows, wondered what they were teaching her. And I realized that, in a predictable turn of events, I'd begun to care for her.

Of course, we watch Sesame Street, too. Some of the jokes are for adults more than kids, but one thing that Emma and I enjoy equally is the interplay between Elmo and one of his friends, Zoe. Zoe has a pet rock named "Rocko." She treats Rocko as though he's a real, sentient presence. Although Elmo is, generally speaking, upbeat and helpful, one of his primary purposes is just to be nice and patient to everyone who comes to Sesame Street, he gets very annoyed by Zoe's insistence that Rocko has thoughts and emotions. When I caught that she and I were both laughing at this, I assumed that I knew the real, deeper reason for the laughter. I thought I understood the full irony of the situation. But I watch Emma laugh not at Zoe, not at the deadpan of the rock, but at Elmo's annoyance, and I realize that even after all my education, basically, we're laughing at the same thing. Which is at least kind of beautiful.

Mr. Potatohead

Matt hated the closet. The smooth glide of the doors didn't fit with the lies and frustration inside. The dozen or so shirts he regularly wore (mostly solid-color polos) were easy to navigate, but the back, where all the funeral/wedding shirts and jackets hung, was difficult to get to. He hadn't worn the ivory shirt since Jesse's funeral, but he hadn't gotten rid of it, either. It hung in their closet; well, his side of the closet. It seemed odd that the shirt had never come up in therapy. Maybe Joan never mentioned the shirt because he kept it where he had to hide his things. It wouldn't have been so bad if he were just hiding something from Joan. Then he could've put it in the basement, behind some tools or in one of the storage bins where he kept the things that were from his father. After all the damned therapy, he had to keep the last toy behind the porn that he had to leave in a place that Joan could find, if she was looking.

She wasn't supposed to look, because part of her therapy was developing her own interests and pulling back so that he could successfully compartmentalize his portion of their lives. Joan had been able to take to the therapy without having to compartmentalize like Matt did, although Matt knew that he was supposed to respect and not resent that. He wondered if she did look, though, trying to discern his taste. These concerns made him buy regular, one-on-one pornography instead of exploring some of the specialty magazines, like the showering Asian women or orgy-based ones. He thought that the Asian ones might've been okay, but that the orgy ones might've been too joyful to be part of a legitimate self project. It made him hate Masturbation Therapy.

He cleared his throat a little as he moved the small box of porn out of the way to look down at the remnants of his dead son's toy. It could've been a present they were hiding for Christmas. He remembered watching it turn in the microwave. It didn't really melt; it more folded in on itself, too flimsy for an outside without anything inside. The fold had started slowly, then taken a quick, comical turn where the melting eyes crossed, and the face looked grumpy. This had been in the middle of Erasure Therapy, when the taboo had been broken and there still seemed to be a lot of toys left. It was exciting in its own way, but it was shortly after Mr. Potatohead that Matt recognized the finite supply, and he had dug it out of the garbage.

Now, he just stared at it and thought that it should've had a candle inside it, or that it could've been part of an art school kid's thesis. "Modern Masculinity in Three Parts," he mumbled. Maybe Donkey Kong would be Part Two. Matt reached in and touched the half-melted thing; it didn't feel all that different than any other kind of plastic. He should've blown it up with firecrackers like they'd done with the Play-Doh. Though it would've taken a lot of firecrackers. Matt wondered if there was some kind of support group for people going through Erasure Therapy. If there was, the therapist should've mentioned it, and if there wasn't, then what kind of therapy was it? But he couldn't bring that up.

Matt ran his fingers along the ridge of the toy, and then he pushed the box back in front of it. He tilted the cover just a bit. The invite might make Joan less likely to look. Not that it mattered. He closed the closet doors and sat on the bed. He needed to wait a few seconds, then flush the toilet and wash his hands. Joan was making dinner, but she was probably listening. This would set her mind at ease. He bounced on the bed just a little bit, and then he sat for a moment and breathed deeply. He felt a little like passing out. The walls looked bare after they'd taken all the family photos down. After Jesse's death, the therapist had said they should take down the pictures one each week to balance moving on with reducing the sense of shock. It had worked, for the most part, but now, as he looked at the walls, he had no idea who he and Joan were or what they liked. There had been a time when he couldn't have imagined not having some band's poster on his wall, but he generally didn't listen to the bands whose posters he owned anymore.

Matt stood slowly, hoping not to feel woozy. After standing for a few seconds, he felt steady enough to go to the bathroom. The bathroom's theme was green this week. The towels and toilet cover, anyway. Matt washed his hands and dried them on the guest towel. He smoothed it out and scratched at his chin. He and Joan had tried to keep up with their personal maintenance so that people would ask them how they were doing less than if they looked like hell. Some weeks, though, it felt comforting to indulge in a little self-neglect, which the therapist said that they could do, but sparingly. Some weeks Joan and Matt had unspoken competitions to see who would sleep less. Matt thought he was winning this week, having several nights of staying up to watch awful, old horror movies on TV. At about four-and-a-half hours per night, he had the satisfaction of the weary, but he wasn't sure if Joan was playing. She'd only had half a cup of coffee this morning.

Matt went downstairs and immediately smelled the chicken. Joan had taken really well to cooking the grown-up dinners so that they could live the life of the fully realized. He wondered if they'd have the larger, chewier garlic bread or the thinner, crispier bread. He liked the chewier, but Joan liked the crispier. Jesse had liked the chewier, though he'd eat either kind. Matt walked over to the kitchen, where his wife was chopping carrots. There was a growing pile next to an already cut pile of celery. The peppers were still whole. "Looks good," he said. Joan smiled at him, then went back to chopping. He wished that she'd listen to music or watch TV while she did this. Since they'd destroyed all the toys and gotten rid of most of the photos, they were supposed to begin doing things like listening to their music and watching their movies more. But it was hard to accurately remember a life before Jesse. Matt went to the dining room window and looked at the yard. They'd have to rake that weekend. After Jesse's death, Matt hated housework more than he did before or during Jesse's life. He wanted to move into a condo complex, but he didn't know how to even bring that up with Joan. It would, of course, require therapist input, which could taint the whole move.

"You want some wine?" Matt asked. Joan finished the carrots and slid the leftover tops into the trash. "With dinner," she said. Matt nodded and went to the living room. He sat on the couch and looked at the TV, dark and blank. The last good day he could remember having with Joan was when they'd grilled the

Transformers over margaritas. The backlog of toys had seemed infinite then. It was probably five minutes before he should start pouring the wine and setting the table. The living room, unlike their bedroom, had some decorations, mostly nature pictures and some bland fake plants. He was okay with the wreathes, but the branches with berries bothered him for some reason. After a minute or so, he took out his cell phone, lost two hands of poker, and then picked a few bits of lint off his shirt. His reflection in the TV seemed to have a too-small head. It must've had something to do with the curvature of the screen. He thought of the melted potato-head upstairs, hidden and useless, but nothing he could part with. He wished they'd donated the toys to charity, but the therapist had advised against it. Still, dumping melted plastic into their garbage bin was depressing, like a hangover.

With nothing better to do, Matt went to the kitchen and took a bottle of wine down from the cupboard. He opened the bottle and took out two glasses. Part of the problem was not being able to go back. In a different life, he'd be drinking fine wine only, and he'd smell the aroma, appreciating it before he appreciated it. In another different life, he'd drink anything, wine or beer or liquor, but be so exhausted by the time he had some, he'd be happy just to be having some kind of booze. As it was, he recognized they could have better, but he wasn't all that sure that he cared that he was drinking something subpar anymore. Even with what the therapist said, it was hard to tell the difference between depression and acceptance. Matt poured a little more in the first glass in order to make sure that the glasses were even. He took the glasses to the dining room table and set them down. Then he went back for the silverware. Probably they could do everything they needed to do with a fork, but he took out two of everything. Sometimes the extra dishes were helpful. It occupied a bit more time. As he set his knife on the table, he spun it a bit, then stopped it with a spoon. There was a dull clang, and he set everything straight. He went back to the kitchen and put plates down by the stove. "How was work?" he asked.

Joan frowned a minute, then started plating the meal. Chicken first. "Decent. I think Danielle is sleeping with Andy."

"Oh," said Matt. He tried to think of who Danielle would be, but could call up neither a face nor a job title. Andy was the office manager, though it seemed like he might've slept around before. Matt tried to remember how Joan had indicated an office affair when Jesse was in the room. "How can you tell?"

Joan chuckled. "She's started filing her nails at her desk." She put down some green beans and some potatoes on both plates. The potatoes did look good. He wondered if therapy would eventually require them to worry about their weight. Strategic Motion Therapy had been awkward and made him too aware of their bodies. They could, conceivably, have another child, but he couldn't imagine having that conversation. "I never see her do much anymore," said Joan.

Matt wondered how old Danielle was. As a child, would she have played with Barbie, Beanie Babies, or would she have been old enough to have played with Strawberry Shortcake in her original run? "Think anything'll come of it?"

Joan exhaled. "God, I hope not." She dumped the salad fixings into bowls, then topped them with a little cheese, croutons and some dressing. Italian tonight, which was fine with Matt. He didn't like French, but otherwise most dressings were of roughly the same quality to him. The dressing made him think of the conjunction of pornography and women serving food. It seemed to be more about dominance than general indulgence. The idea that a woman would always want to serve a man in every way. Matt had seen that kind of porn in looking at possible magazines, but he never really enjoyed it. He didn't think he'd get into BDSM even if he and Joan weren't together. As he took the plates over to the dining room, Matt felt a soft panic about how they'd fill dinner time. After months of therapy and trying to work through their grief, they still hadn't really landed anywhere. Neither bottoming out nor finding a clear passion or purpose. He tried to think of what he'd seen on TV or heard on the radio. Aside from his tiny head on the screen, it seemed to be the same as ever, financial worries, inept politicians, and divorcing celebrities. There didn't seem to be anything to latch onto. When they sat down, he began to cut his chicken. As he took a bite, it was moist and warm, a pleasant, subtle flavor. Not the usual overdose of rosemary that Joan could resort to when she was trying to feel like she'd flavored the meal. Matt peeked over at Joan a bit to see if she was watching him. She had her face turned towards her plate, which made Matt assume she was paying close attention to what he was doing. He looked back at his plate as well. As he stabbed a potato, he said, "I think I'll destroy my golf clubs."

There was a long pause. Matt tried to tell if the low whine he heard was real or just his ears straining for something. Eventually, Joan said, "Why is that?". Her voice was a little high, but slow and even. Matt bit his potato and chewed, wondering what his argument would be. Hearing her question, it struck him that he wasn't even sure what response he wanted. The therapist might've said that he was making his grief his own by challenging the boundaries of mourning. Or maybe the therapist wouldn't have yielded that much power. "Well," he said. "They're really not what I want. It was a getaway or a break, and I don't really care for it anymore."

Joan stirred her salad, which was unnecessary. "You could stick them in the garage, in case you wanted them later."

Matt found himself becoming angry. He broke his bread again. It was the crusty kind. "I guess it'll help me to start something new, which is what I want."

Joan picked up her wine glass, swallowed her food and took a small sip. She chewed some more and then said, "What do you have in mind?"

Matt brushed off his hands. "Never mind."

There was very soft scraping on the plate, then Joan quietly said, "Don't pout."

Matt held his glass by the stem and rotated it, watching the surface of his wine ripple. "Things aren't working."

Joan picked her fork back up, but didn't actually put it to use. "Remember that the therapy takes time. We still might be able to reestablish our regular social and sexual patterns if we just stick to the program."

Matt closed his eyes. That phrasing, social and sexual patterns was very obviously from the therapists. He almost said, "Maybe I should take up water colors instead," but he knew that would be petty. Breathing deeply, he felt like the room was starting to tilt slightly, and he had to open his eyes. Joan was gently stabbing a green bean. The fork clicked onto the plate. "Let me do something quick," Matt said. He got up and went to the basement. It was cool and smelled just a bit musty. It smelled like something his parents could've named, but Matt couldn't settle on anything. He grabbed a pair of hedge clippers and took out his nine iron. He put the club between his legs and tried to cut the handle off. The handles wouldn't budge. Matt rearranged his grip, holding them thumb side up so that he could get a bit more leverage. He pushed as hard as he could, and it still didn't move at all. He tried to remember what the salesman had told him about the club's shaft. It felt so light. He set down the clippers and took the club from between his legs. He set the club on his workshop's counter, and he picked up a hammer. He put one knee on the handle, feeling the hard, focused pain of the club interrupting the dull support of the table, and then started to beat the club. His first swing glanced off and did very little. His second landed squarely, but shot pain up his leg without leaving any kind of dent. He took the club to a wall, leaned the club against it and tried jumping onto it to get it to break. The club shot out and he almost fell over. He wished that Joan had come down. She knew to run over Jesse's bicycle with the SUV instead of taking all day beating it with a hammer. Having gone this far, he didn't want to go back upstairs without at least bending it. He looked around at the tools and tried to think. How he could melt, not destroy a plastic figure, but not do any kind of damage to a long, narrow stick was agonizing. Matt picked up the club and twirled it in his hands. He watched the head rotate, and he started to cry. Not a loud sob, but a quiet, convulsing type of cry. He had reached a point of actually feeling good in his tears, feeling like he had landed somewhere when Joan came down. He covered his face but didn't stop crying. Matt dimly noticed her touching his shoulder, and he leaned towards her. She put her arms around him, and he let himself go, though he couldn't tell if she was crying with him or not.

Eulogy

Kelly hated giving the damn eulogy as it was; it was even dumber to have that rickety coffin as a reminder. She'd be the first to admit that the rest of the family's living room furniture wasn't elegant or ornate, but that stupid coffin that Jack had made and was lying in looked tacky to her. Spooky almost, with its plain, unvarnished wood. Like an old timey movie prop. Especially like a Western where the hero was looking at his dead friend or mentor or something right before he went off to get revenge. Kelly wasn't much for revenge, and Jack would only push for it if there was some tangible reward. A settlement that could beef up the kids' college fund, maybe. Like if he'd gotten cancer from asbestos.

That's how Kelly's husband was: a perfectionist. He'd made this lousy coffin mostly by himself (Little Jack wasn't allowed to use power tools yet, but he could hammer some) and it had only taken him the one afternoon. It was sturdy enough to hold him, but nothing to look at, for sure. They'd put a blanket on the bottom so he wouldn't get any splinters or a sore back from lying in it, and that was it. Kelly told him to decorate it, maybe a little bit of etching or dowels for handles. Jack said that was silly. Instead, he'd used the leftover dowels to build a DVD rack, which was handy, Kelly had to admit.

She looked at the lousy coffin, looked at Little Jack fidgeting in his little suit and Susie slouching in her plain dress, and she lost her place in the eulogy Jack wrote for her. She knew she'd mentioned Jack being a good provider, but couldn't remember whether or not she'd gotten past his high school days to the part about him having the foresight to read bedtime stories to Little Jack so that Little Jack could do well in college. To be honest, Kelly didn't like all that. She felt it was too much pressure on a five-year old. He might go to a trade school, for all they knew, and putting his college career right there in the eulogy was basically dooming Little Jack to a specific track of study. "He was…" she stammered, "Jack was…"

"Hey!" Jack said, lifting himself up in his coffin. "Don't pick your nose, Little Jack. This is going to be Daddy's funeral. You're not supposed to pick your nose at Daddy's funeral."

Little Jack's hand dropped down to his knee. "Jack," Kelly said. Both Jack and Little Jack looked over at her.

Jack put his hands over the edge of the coffin. "You were doing so well, Buddy. Just remember, people will be watching. Now do you guys wanna start from the greeting, or from the eulogy?"

Both the kids looked at the floor and said, "Eulogy."

Kelly was grateful for that much. She hated watching the kids go through this. Besides, it was hot today. Kelly was surprised Jack wasn't complaining, being cooped up in the coffin with that heavy blanket. It was one from his grandmother. Maybe she could talk him into stopping if it got hot enough. He wouldn't want to be drained for work on Monday. Though Jack also might have made a point to tough it out.

"Jack, maybe we should take a break."

Jack's jaw dropped. Kelly quickly looked from him to the kids. They were both fidgeting, but she could tell that at least Susie was paying attention to see if Kelly could actually stop a rehearsal when Jack wanted to keep going.

"No, Kelly," said Jack. "I could just as easily die in the summer as I could in the winter, and what then? Besides, the kids were doing well until you lost your place in the eulogy."

"Well…I could become overwhelmed with emotion. Shouldn't they be prepared for that?" She saw Jack nodding and felt bad for putting the kids back in the spotlight. Little Jack didn't notice, he was playing with his tie, but Susie was already shaking her head and rolling her eyes before Jack's response. Susie had figured out that Jack was pretty predictable, and Kelly hated it when Jack proved Susie right.

"Your mom has a point, you know," said Jack.

"What if she dies first?" asked Susie. "Or if I do? Of boredom"

"Don't get smart," said Jack. As glad as Kelly was that Susie got yelled at for that crack, she did worry about what would happen if she died first. Jack didn't always get the kids' emotions the way that a dad should. She didn't want them to grow up to be robots, or heartless CEOs. But that's what efficiency and practicality could get you. Jack was just on the good side of being a human being. When the two of them first started living together, Jack would explain the things he did, like that he set aside one day a month to be a crying day, because he generally didn't cry, but he felt he should now and then. By then Kelly was getting used to his quirks, so she took it in stride, but with kids around, she liked this less and less.

Kelly sighed and scratched the back of her neck. She thought that most funeral parlors would be air conditioned so the mourners wouldn't sweat.

"I hope Charlie won't give the eulogy if I can't."

"Excuse me?" Jack said. His brother could be a sore spot, but Kelly probably shouldn't have said it out loud.

"Jack," Kelly said. "We're all hot."

Jack smiled at the kids. "As soon as we get done, we can dress down and have some funeral pie."

"Whoopee," said Susie, slumping even further down in her chair. Her legs were splayed a little too far open, but Kelly didn't want to say anything during a rehearsal. One of the awful, grown-up facts that Susie was realizing was that she'd never be model beautiful, and Kelly felt for her. Of course, being just nice looking instead of beautiful could be a good thing. It meant less pressure. Kelly thought of herself as nice looking.

"Maybe I should check on the pie," offered Susie.

Jack looked down at his watch. "It'll be a while yet, Sweetie."

Susie sighed loud enough to show that she knew what she was doing. Little Jack had twisted his tie to almost backwards. "Is Daddy going to die soon, Mommy?"

Kelly walked over to Little Jack and fixed his tie. "No," she said, "Daddy is fine. He just had a physical in May."

Little Jack struggled a bit, just enough to show he was unhappy, but he still let her get the tie back to hanging down his front. Little Jack was a good kid. Jack had put in a lot of time training him how to behave, but they were playing with fire by making him sit still for so long.

"We never know when I could die," Jack said. "Death and taxes, Kelly."

"Can I die soon?" Susie said.

Jack started to open his mouth, but Kelly shook her head, and he actually stopped. "Stop it," said Kelly. "Let's all stop it. We can cut the eulogy short and just do the songs and the commitment of the remains to the earth."

"Already?" Jack asked.

Kelly felt bad enough for making everyone in her extended family sit through a traditional wedding, but she'd let Jack's family have their way. She wanted the funerals at least to go quickly for anyone who was still around by the time she and Jack died. "Oh God, Jack, are we training them to behave during the funeral, or are we training them to hate family activities?"

Jack just stared at Kelly for a few seconds, and then he said, "Fine. We can stop for today, but I don't want to make a habit of just giving up on the funerals."

Kelly wished she had a drink in her hand. A good, solid tumbler that she could drain and slam on a table or their mantel to mark her frustration. Kelly rubbed her eyes. There was an awful headache coming on.

"Can I unbutton my shirt?" asked Little Jack.

"No," said Jack immediately. "Do you know what Grandma and Grandpa would say? Or Auntie Jean? You can't take off the tie at the funeral, so you can't take it off right now."

Little Jack started to cry. Just a showy cry at first. "It's okay," Kelly said. "As soon as the songs are done, we can have pie."

"But I'm hot," Little Jack said.

Susie picked at her nails and said "We're all hot." She looked over at Kelly. Kelly didn't feel much allegiance to Susie. Love, but not allegiance. She'd been such a pain in the ass these last few years.

"We should do some weeping drills today," said Jack. "Maybe in the afternoon after pie. Some of last weekend's sobs sounded a lot like coughs."

"Jack, let's focus on right now."

Jack slid all the way to the back of the coffin, resting a little bit on the headboard. Kelly didn't think it could support all his weight. If the conversation kept going long enough, he'd have to get out. It would be just like Jack to start fixing it if he heard any kind of a creak.

"I already cried this week anyway," Susie said. She was running her finger along the little gold chain they'd asked her to wear. Susie'd drawn the line at putting on the cross they bought for her, and Kelly was okay with that.

"You cried?" Kelly asked.

"I don't like the weeping drills." Little Jack started kicking his heels against his chair's legs.

Kelly shushed him and hugged him to her. "Why were you crying, Susie?"

Susie straightened up a little, but her face still looked like slouching. "Because Tim Jorgenson is an asshole."

"Susie!" Kelly rubbed Little Jack's back, trying to distract him. She could feel how hot the little guy was even through the jacket.

"Little Jack," said Jack from the coffin, "that's a word your sister shouldn't have said, and you should never repeat it. Okay, Bud?"

Little Jack said, "'Kay." He was watching something either crawling on the wall or moving right outside the window. Kelly couldn't see it.

"What happened with Tim Jorgenson?" asked Kelly. Susie kept her eyes half lidded and peeked over towards Jack. Jack had his arms crossed. Susie wouldn't talk in front of him. "Did he do something to you?" Jack asked.

Little Jack was starting to tug on Kelly's blouse, and that meant real tears weren't far off. Still, she and Jack had agreed that they had to show Susie that she was just as important as Little Jack so that she didn't resent having a brother who was so much younger. Susie would never have admitted to her or Jack that she wanted their attention, but Kelly could tell there'd been jealousy. "Do you want us to talk to Tim's parents or the principal?"

"No. God, Mom."

"Honey," said Jack, "Do we need to put you in a private school? St. Joe's has a reputation for excellence."

Little Jack was starting to squirm, now. Kelly decided that the focus was off of him enough that she could loosen his tie.

"You're not even Catholic, Dad," said Susie.

Jack put his hands on his lower back and stretched. He looked towards the ceiling, or tilted his head back, anyway. Kelly finished loosening Little Jack's tie and then sat him back in the chair. She tried to muss his hair, but he just pulled away and crossed his arms.

"You know," said Jack, "Craig Anderson's family isn't Catholic, and he still goes to St. Joe's."

"Let's not have this argument today," said Kelly. "And that is a legitimate thing to say, because I might be saying it on the day of your funeral if I have to deal with stuff like this."

Jack frowned, but didn't say anything back. Susie got that satisfied look on her face and Kelly wanted to slap her for it. "Let's go straight to the burial, and, Susie, you and I can talk about Tim Jorgenson later."

Nobody seemed particularly happy with that decision, but everyone must've known better than to start up again, because Jack and Susie both just sighed. They were moving into a line to pretend that they were singing when the phone rang. Jack frowned at Kelly and said, "We'll wait, but make it quick."

Kelly waited until she was in the kitchen before she cursed under her breath. The caller ID identified her mother. The caller ID actually said "Foley, Ed," which was her dad's name, but Kelly knew it was her mother. She took a deep breath and answered. "Hi, Mom."

"Hi, Kel. How are you doing?"

Kelly looked down at the receiver. On a cordless phone, there was nothing to pling. "Okay. A little busy."

"Did I call at a bad time, Sweetie?"

Kelly turned on the oven light and tried to see how brown the crust was, but the crappy light in the oven and the darkness of the door made it too close to call. "No, I'm just a little busy is all."

Kelly's mom got that tone in her voice. Not annoyed, but like hunkering down. "I won't hold you then. It's just that I know Little Jack's birthday is coming up, and you never gave me a list of toys for him is all."

Kelly played with her bangs the way that she knew she always had as a teenager. "I know, Mom. I'll send you an e-mail really soon, I promise. Things have just been a little crazy here. You know how it is."

There was a really quick pause. "Is Susie in some kind of trouble?"

Kelly closed her eyes. She never knew how much to tell her mother. Maybe she should've blamed Susie today. "No, Mom. Things are fine; they're just busy. Send me an e-mail and I'll remember to send you the list. Really."

"Please don't send it as an attachment, Kelly. You know our computer has problems. Your brother tried to show me how to do it, but I might not have the programs or something."

"Okay, Mom." Kelly didn't mind being away from the living room, but she knew that things would deteriorate if she stayed in the kitchen too long.

"Kel," said her mom. "Is something going on between you and Jack?"

Kelly pressed her palm against her head. "We're rehearsing the funeral today."

"Oh," said Kelly's mom. "Again?"

"I know it seems weird, but if I give a little on this, then Jack eases off on other stuff. You know how it is."

Kelly's mom chuckled. "I know about compromise. Funeral practice, not so much."

Kelly picked at her fingernails and didn't say anything. Her mother broke the silence. "He's been very good to you and the kids. And I know your father had his projects and ideas. When you guys—"

Jack yelled, "The kids are getting hot, Kel."

Kelly yelled back, "It's my mother," forgetting to cover the mouthpiece. Her mother wouldn't say anything about the yelling, but it was still a little embarrassing. She couldn't hear exactly what Jack said back, but she knew the gist of it from experience and tone. She wished that she could tell both of them to leave her alone so

she could check the pie for real. Baking was one of the mother/
wife things that she actually liked to do.

"I've gotta go, Mom."

"Just remember, we let you be kids, and you all turned out okay."

Kelly sighed and laughed. "I love you, Mom."

"Thanks, dear. I love you, too."

As Kelly hung up, she remembered what her mother had always
told her about sex. "It's how some people like to touch their hearts".
Just three times in, Kelly laughed during sex, because she couldn't
stop thinking about her mom's saying. Ricky Johnson, her sort-of
partner, didn't think it was funny. He'd wanted to do something
where their hearts were not going to touch, and Kelly laughed
when he asked her for a new position while they were having normal sex. Sometimes, Kelly hated life.

"I'll be back in a minute," Kelly yelled to the family. She opened
the oven door and stood back to avoid that first blast of hot air.
When she squatted down and peeked in, she saw that the insides
were bubbling and the crust was basically golden brown. "Good
enough," as her father would've said. She took the pie out of the
oven and set it on a trivet to cool.

As she looked at the pie, she wondered if this was how the
children would remember their childhood. Kelly took out the
pie plates, that little knife/spatula thing for serving, and the ice
cream scoop. In a minute or two, she'd take the ice cream out to
let it soften, but the pie had to cool down for quite a bit yet. They
had French vanilla for Susie, and New York vanilla for Little
Jack. Kelly wasn't a big fan of ice cream in general. On a day like
today, she'd really just as soon have some watermelon anyway.

But she and Jack liked to give the kids some kind of stability, and apple pie was the regular funeral pie, and their apple pie was à la mode.

As she got out the napkins and forks, she wondered who had to coordinate baking and cooking for the bereaved family so they didn't end up getting a bunch of the same casseroles or breads and stuff. Kelly didn't want to be in charge of all that if Jack went first, and it seemed rude to ask people to make specific things, although Jack might if Kelly went first, because that's just how his mind worked. That's how he'd comfort the kids. If they were grown up, he'd probably delegate to them. Which wasn't the worst thing. At least they'd have something to feel in control with.

Kelly got the pie ready, and she realized that they'd never properly celebrated Jack's last promotion or two. They'd both been so expected that Jack just took her and the kids out for a nice dinner and then went back home. Going on a vacation or even a hotel for the weekend had never come up as a possibility. It was like she'd been cheated by her husband's competence.

Little Jack shuffled into the kitchen. "Mommy? Can you help me take off my jacket?"

"Of course," said Kelly. "Didn't Daddy help you take it off?"

Little Jack played with his tie again. "I don't like Daddy when he's in the coffin."

Kelly patted his head, took off his jacket, and unbuttoned his shirt a little. "You should tell him that, Sweetie." She wished that she didn't have to use Little Jack's fears as leverage to have fewer of these funeral rehearsals. But Jack may have sent the little guy into the kitchen to move things along in the first place. That's how things ran during times of struggle. Kelly kissed Little Jack's sweaty head. "That better, Jack?"

"Yep." He looked tired. Kelly hoped he didn't start getting nightmares from all this. She didn't want them to push the kids too hard, and she felt bad always making Jack be the hardass.

Kelly tickled his belly and Little Jack smiled. "Tell you what," she said. "Why don't you go get your sister and Daddy, and we can all have pie now and do the weeping drills a little later." If Jack couldn't say no to Kelly directly, he always said yes for some reason. Or maybe it was the power of her and Little Jack put together. She'd never try it with Susie anymore.

"'Kay," said Little Jack. He tromped into the living room. Kelly went back to the table. The pie would just have to be cool enough. And the ice cream would help. Jack liked to eat his pie in vertical segments, plowing straight through from front to crust. Kelly liked to let the ice cream and sweet insides pool up together. She'd noticed Susie watching her and Jack eat pie once. When Susie picked up her fork and went to take a bite, Kelly forced herself to look away. Some things weren't worth worrying about.

Disposal

Most of the kids would start the day with a Kahlua and cream or a cheap beer, then switch over to black Russians after dinner, when real drinking was acceptable. Their mother had created a huge stash of alcohol over the years, and they had to get rid of it. But the oldest two stayed away from the Kahlua. Barbara and Charlie were more no-nonsense, dipping into the gin right off the bat. Barbara with some tonic water and a little Rose's lime, Charlie for martinis, though he at least knew to pace himself. Even having worked for half a week and having given some of the odd bottles to the neighbors, there was still plenty. Their mother had been a good hostess. That also meant that she had a lot of friends in the park. All retirees as their mother was, and the kids appreciated that the neighbors came around; it justified their breaks and made their drinking social.

But they did throw things out when people weren't around. Laminated frogs propped up to look like a mariachi band, an armadillo statue curled around an empty bottle of tequila. Things she must've bought while she was as drunk as the kids were as they threw it out. "American vices propping up the Mexican economy," said Andrea. The rest of the kids made grunts and continued working, though Danny made a jerk-off motion.

Mostly, the nasty little knick-knacks they found got a laugh or two, a trip around the condo so that each kid could see it, and a final toss into a large, black trash bag. Barbara to Charlie to Andrea to Danny to Tom to Gwen to Kristi to the garbage. Though not always in that order, and they sometimes were resurrected from the trash. Now and then, Kristi would stash something in one of the houseplants. None of the kids had noticed how many there were when they'd gone to visit one at a time, but now it struck each of them that there were a lot of the plants. Nobody had brought up what to do with them, though. Not the car, either. A Trans-Am that the grandkids would've drooled over, which was a central part of the problem.

As the children were passing around a Day-of-the-Dead bus complete with skeletons, Jeannie Brown showed up with some buns and a large bucket full of barbecue. She volunteered that she'd been there when their mother had bought the bus, and very little else was said. But the kids did appreciate the barbecue. While helping to serve, Barbara told Jeannie that she always remembered her barbecue as the best in the neighborhood, which was a high compliment where they'd grown up. Jeannie smiled at the kids. They offered her a drink, but she said she had to see the Wendt's before they headed across the border for the day.

After she left, the kids agreed that they didn't remember much about Jeannie Brown. As a family with a pool, they'd rarely met the other moms in the neighborhood. Danny said that he remembered pushing around her son during wrestling practice. That was about it. But it was nice to have a connection to their original home. Maybe Jeannie had been one of the folks who'd talked their mother into being a Winter Texan. She'd always appreciated the warm climate and the easy access to a permissive brand of Catholicism. None of the kids really practiced, although Gwen talked about God a lot. Danny had stuck a little Jesus statue into a Christmas cactus's dirt.

***

It was on the fourth day that the bickering really started. Kristi wanted to have a rummage sale right there in the complex. She said that their mother's friends would like the fun of buying her trinkets. "It'd be like one last shopping trip," she said. Charlie said that it'd be a waste of a day, though he might've had other objections in mind. Barbara said that it would be too morbid, though there might've been other objections there, too. Or the same objections, but thought of differently. Kristi had been holding a clay ashtray shaped like a pig when she proposed it, which didn't really help her cause. Behind Kristi's back, Andrea said that Kristi was probably just strapped for cash, which may have been true, but she shouldn't have said it.

The real trouble, though, came when Ross, their mother's third grandkid and Barbara's most fucked-up son (no small accomplishment there), showed up clearly drunk and wearing mesh shorts, a wife beater and dreadlocks. Ross had been close with their mother, maybe closer than some of the kids themselves, but they all, except for Barbara, had gotten too many calls from their mother about Ross showing up in the middle of the night and making noise or too artlessly hitting on neighbors' kids and grandkids. They also knew, though their mother never said it, that Ross had put some of her jewelry into hock, albeit with her blessing. Not the gaudy stuff she'd buy in Mexico, either. While Ross was babbling to Barbara, Charlie said that their mother had probably given Ross his first drink. "Circle of life," said Danny, but neither of the other boys laughed.

Barbara never said much of anything about her son. She'd married a drunk. When they got divorced, everyone told her that it skipped a generation. It didn't. Or maybe it did, but there were just always enough drunks from his family to not let any of the kids skate through.

Most of the kids just kept throwing out junk. All the while, Ross was crying on the couch. He was snuggling an aloe vera plant. Now and then, he'd break off a leaf and rub it on a scrape or a burn that nobody would ask him about. The kids all kept working in silence, drinking. Ross would ask his mother for his drink, now and then. "In a minute, Honey," Barbara would say, "in a minute."

Between Ross making his last trip to the bottles at 6:00 and passing out by 8:00, he didn't get off the couch. On that last trip, he knocked down a vase that some combination of the kids had bought their mother. They started arguing again, first about whether or not Ross should've been there at all, and then about which of the kids had chipped in for the vase all those years ago. Danny, who was well beyond drunk himself at that point, smashed the stand that the vase had been on. That brought on an awkward silence and a sudden bedtime. The aloe vera sat alone by the side of the couch. Gwen made a show of praying for the family.

The next day, Barbara sent Ross over to the Beards. The Beards were newer to the complex, so they weren't aware of his history. Ross hadn't been around as much once their mother fell sick, which the kids thought was shitty, but none of them actually said it out loud. The Beards were also "nice folks". They could be trusted to slow down Ross's drinking while keeping pace themselves. The kids would have a chance to keep cleaning in relative peace. There was still some tension after the broken vase. For whatever reason, no one moved the aloe plant.

The kids had decided that they'd mail some things back home that day, and that meant that someone had to stay sober long enough to drive in to town and mail out the boxes. Tom volunteered, but some of the other children insisted that they all draw straws. Gwen got the short one.

Tom would stay sober enough to help carry the boxes, but he still needed to drink enough to seem sociable. The kids broke into the usual groups: Andrea and Kristi took turns talking to Barbara and not talking to Barbara. When either of them was away from Barbara, they said that Ross should've been sent to Mass, and then to the post office, because it would cut down on the trouble. When they were with Barbara, either one of them would say, "Luck of the draw." Neither of them said anything to Gwen or Tom. Danny, Charlie, and Tom all just joked around. Gwen was humming.

After he noticed that Tom was nursing his drinks, Danny started mixing a few for Tom, and he mixed them strong. Charlie just drank and laughed and joked. By the early afternoon, they all agreed that it was time to break for lunch and then send Gwen and Tom off to the post office. Tom's face was flushed. He asked for a highball. Danny said he'd do it, but Charlie got up first and said, "I'll do it, Tom." Danny shrugged. If he had still smoked, he might've lit up a cigarette then.

During lunch, Danny's wife called. None of them had made a real effort to be close with her, though most of the children couldn't have given a good reason why. Danny had his guesses, knowing both his wife and siblings well enough.

When he went to the phone, the rest of the children giggled without having to make any particular joke. They'd settled down by the time he came back, which was good, because he came back in a bad mood. Kristi tried bringing up the plants, but nobody would answer her. The lunch was mostly eaten by then anyway, so everyone broke back into their groups. Danny ate by himself in the kitchen and Tom decided to take a mug of coffee with him when he and Gwen left. Most of the children gradually helped to load the car. Kristi watered the plants. Danny still had a sandwich in his hand. His second.

By the time the car was ready, Tom was dripping with sweat, although the boxes actually weren't all that heavy. "Not used to the heat," he said. As the children got closer to finishing, they got less and less productive. Kristi and Andrea talked about whose old boyfriends were doing what now. Neither of them had dated anyone who'd ended up much of a success, although Kirsti claimed that her junior prom date had a bit part in Beverly Hills Cop. Barbara simply nodded at that. Gwen never involved herself with boyfriend conversations; she would've whistled or hummed if she'd been there. Danny stewed and drank. He went over to the couch and snapped off a leaf from the aloe plant, then realized that he really didn't know what to do next. He sniffed it, then threw it out.

When Gwen and Tom got back, neither of them had a thing to say to the other children. Even when the children tried one by one to talk to them, Gwen and Tom kept quiet. The only thing that could be confirmed was that Tom came back without his coffee mug. That night, Ross came back, too. He brought out some pot and told everyone that he would've given it to his grandmother if she'd still been alive. "For the chemo," he said. "Or radiation or whatever." She'd given up on treatment a couple of months before she died.

Ross sipped tequila while he rolled a joint. He took a couple more sips of tequila, then staggered off to bed without smoking up. The kids giggled a little as they took the joint off the counter, and then passed it around while rolling another one. Barbara poured out the tequila Ross hadn't finished. "Hey," said Andrea, "someone else could've drunk that."

"There's two more bottles under the sink," said Barbara. Things got quiet again. After about twenty minutes of good work, they finished all the frozen pizzas that were supposed to last the next two days, and then they played half a game of cards. The drinking had slowed down, and they were all fairly docile. Danny went to get a little more of Ross's stash, and he came back in ten minutes, unable to find anything. Barbara piped up. "Ross can drive the Trans Am back, and we can load it up with the house plants." Nobody said anything, which counted as a vote. Barbara won the next hand and the kids trickled off to bed to think or pass out.

The children woke up with only mild hangovers. But they were still quiet. There was just that day and the next, and then they'd have to head home. Almost everything was done. Mostly just cleaning left. There was still some old furniture to send to Goodwill. There was a discussion about drawing straws again, but eventually they all decided that the boys would move the furniture and the girls would clean. Barbara talked Ross into just going home. When he'd gotten up, Barbara took him aside. He just nodded the whole time, then made coffee and went to do yoga in an empty room, but Danny said he just said that so he could have a room to beat off in. Either way, the kids left him alone.

The boys headed off to pick up the U-Haul truck, and they got through the first load without any trouble. Not even a scrape on the walls. One bent chair leg, but nothing broken. Danny shrugged. "Beggars can't be choosers," which Andrea would later tell Kristi was a tasteless thing to say about Goodwill. "I know," Kristi would say back. As they left, Ross brought the first two plants to the Trans Am: a spider plant and the aloe. While the boys were gone, Ross watered the rest and covered the car's seats with newspaper the kids had been using to wrap things.

When the boys came back for the second load, they brought in a case of beer. The girls complained about this. "You spent money on beer?" asked Kristi.

"It was out of our own pockets," explained Charlie.

"You're not going to return the truck to U-Haul drunk, are you?" asked Andrea.

"We'll be fine," said Tom.

"Are you doing your best, sober job cleaning?" asked Danny.

Everyone quieted down, drank, and did their jobs. Ross had added a Christmas cactus, another spider plant, and some plant that none of them could identify. It had yellow flowers all over, like a rash. Andrea and Kristi, who both knew where Ross kept his pot, found he'd taken it all with him when he left. They threw out the crossword puzzle books in silence. After the boys drove off with the second and final load, the girls broke for lunch. They each had a Bloody Mary. At first, they talked about how some of the furniture was bound to get bent and scraped to make it in just two loads. Later, they talked, for the first time on the trip, about the fact that Charlie was named as executor of the will. Kristi and Andrea both told Barbara that she should've been executor, Gwen would only say, "It definitely shouldn't have been Charlie."

Barbara shrugged and turned her hands in the air. "He's the oldest male child, I guess."

Ross walked by with a bonsai tree that he'd place in the passenger's seat.

After that, the girls decided that they needed beer chasers for the rest of their Bloody Marys. "You know, the beer chaser is really a Wisconsin thing," said Kristi.

"Midwestern," said Gwen.

"Oh," said Kristi. "Really?"

Barbara smiled at Gwen. "I've found a bar or two in Illinois that gives you a beer with your Bloody Mary." She winked, and the rest of the girls smiled back.

So they cleaned and drank and talked about the funeral arrangements. Having had a drawn-out bout with cancer, their mother had plenty of time to talk to the kids about funeral, eulogy, who to notify or to snub, and so on. But she'd never gone into the details of the disposal of her remains other than saying that she just wanted to be cremated. When their father had died, it was simple enough to just give their mother the ashes, which she'd sprinkled on some hunting land. But with both parents gone, there wasn't a clear person to divide things, even if Charlie was the executor. For some reason, none of the kids could remember how much ash there was from their father, and nobody thought that their mother would want to be on the hunting land. Ross stopped loading up to eat a salad, then he carried out a rubber tree.

Andrea asked about scattering the ashes in Mexico, and Kristi asked if they'd be able to take ashes across the border. Andrea started to tell a story about one of her husband's uncles smuggling his buddy's ashes inside of a football. "That's stupid," said Gwen. "Someone might have thought the ashes were drugs."

Andrea and Kristi began to sulk. Barbara said, "Well, that's beside the point, anyway. We should scatter the ashes some place that we'll all actually visit."

They all nodded, but nobody put forth a suggestion. It was just quiet. The boys came back laughing. Charlie tossed a plastic bag in the trash. The girls couldn't tell how many empties were in the bag, but there was definitely clanking. Tom brought in a grocery bag. "We can make dinner ourselves tonight."

"What about the mess?" asked Andrea and Kristi.

"We can throw away the pans. There's no point in washing them."

The girls started taking things out of the bag. A can of tomato sauce, parmasean cheese, ground round, eggs. Meatloaf. The girls smiled.

While they were cooking, Ross put the last plant, a lily, into the car. He found a hand spade and went to the front yard to get something else. "Christ," said Kristi.

The kids ignored him. People came in and out of the kitchen, cleaned, and drank. Even after all the drinking, there were still enough bottles that they didn't have to slow down. They sat down to the meatloaf, a little overdone, but that's how most of them liked it. Along with the meatloaf, they had chips and beer. "We should've had potato salad," Tom said. For some reason, everyone laughed.

Ross came in, walking steady and carrying a cake pan full of dirt and little cacti. "I'm ready," he said.

The kids stared until Barbara got up and touched his elbow. "I'll walk you out."

After they got out the front door, the kids stood up and craned their heads to watch. "Bet he doesn't make it home alive," said Danny.

Nobody answered or looked at him. Outside, Barbara kissed Ross on the cheek and he got into the car, disappearing into a miniature jungle, bound for colder states. The kids sat down, trying not to seem nosey. When Barbara got back, they gave her a piece of meatloaf, and that was about it. They did talk about their mom's ashes again. Barbara was starting to go on and on about how to decide where they should put them, and Charlie eventually just said, "Lake Chenequa", then took a huge bite of meatloaf. It wasn't a bad answer, but it wasn't what Barbara had wanted from the conversation. Everyone knew that.

Still, nobody argued. After Ross left, they'd hit that place of caring less, which was the ideal mindset for disposal. It's how things worked, and nobody had a specific objection to Lake Chenequa, no more than Charlie would've had a specific answer, if he'd been asked why. The kids would finish up while Ross took the plants back home or somewhere else. As much of a fuckup as he was, he'd probably put them somewhere that they'd take root.

Volume

lthough Myra and I had discussed this minor problem on several occasions, it was some time before she first made any overt mention of my acting upon the situation. Myra, of course, was the one to first broach the subject. She sat down on my bed while I was reading. She was still wearing her night shirt, which made me position my book strategically over the lower half of my body. I feel that apartmentmates should maintain a certain level of modesty.

To Myra's credit, she at least considered my interest level in her broaching the subject. "Did their music keep you up last night, too?"

I had never had a significant issue with the late night (and eventually early morning) music. Due to my mind's constant activity, I rarely get more than a few hours of sleep anyway, so nocturnal noise is less significant to me than to the average Joe or Joan. The only time it really annoyed me was when it was one of those vaguely recognizable tunes that get played ad nauseum on the radio, but whose title you never bother to learn. Such songs inevitably left me in the fruitless pursuit of a title which I, on some level, knew that I would never be able to produce. Typically some song about women and romance or less noble intentions to which (as might be imagined) I tend not to relate. Some nights I would lie in my bed, in a state of longing, until the dawn found me red-eyed and exasperated. But those occasions were infrequent, and the previous night had not been one of them.

"No," I said in response.

Myra leaned over, supporting herself with one palm. "Really? I couldn't get back to sleep even after I asked them to turn it down a little."

I smoothed the paper out a bit. "Perhaps it was worse on your end of the apartment."

"Should we call the cops next time? They hardly turned it down at all."

I propped a pillow behind my back and avoided eye contact. "Let's talk to them first. They might be reasonable if I ask them nicely."

Myra snorted, but I still did not look at her. "The sorority twins? Unless you can explain how it'll help them put out, they won't be interested."

I frowned and folded my paper. "Well, it'll be at least a few days before they play their music late anyway."

Myra stood up. "So I'm the only one who's going to talk to them?"

I shifted a little against my pillow. "Let's wait and see what happens Thursday or Friday."

***

Thursday night was the one night each week when Myra and I regularly dined together. Other nights would depend upon our outside obligations, but Thursdays, our work and television schedules coincided so that we could sit down and have a meal like a little family. We were having lasagna that night. It was the third week of the cycle that we used for selecting meals. The first week, I would select the meal, the second week, Myra, and the third week, we would choose together. Pasta dishes were typically agreeable, and so I had suggested lasagna. Myra agreed without any protest.

We had both finished our small salads and had moved on to the main course when the music came on. It was a slow and jazzy style that would have ordinarily made for very pleasant mealtime listening. However, given our recent conversations, it added an air of tension to the meal. We sat in silence, except for the music of course, for several minutes, neither of us looking at each other. When I eventually initiated eye contact, Myra's expression made me wish that I'd continued feigning ignorance. "I hear it."

She looked back at her plate. "You don't think it's a little loud?"

I grabbed a piece of garlic bread and began dipping it in the half-eaten portion of my lasagna. "It's still a while before either of us will be going to bed. It isn't interfering with our normal daily activities."

"So you don't find it distracting?"

I took a large bite and spoke through a mouthful of food. "I'm still eating, aren't I?"

She took a sip of wine. "You can eat and listen at the same time, sure. But if you were trying to watch TV, or, oh say, have a conversation, then this would probably get on your nerves."

I took a large drink of water, forcing the half-chewed chunks of bread and lasagna down my throat, almost bringing tears to my eyes. "I've watched the television while they were playing music. In fact, I do it a lot."

She began to run her finger around the rim of her glass. "Oh really? And when you're watching TV, do you imagine them both dancing around in their bra and panties? Hitting each other with pillows and giggling?"

Our neighbors were attractive young coeds of a generally playful nature, but the picture Myra painted with these questions was fair to neither them nor myself. Even if I did plan to pursue any sort of relationship with them (beyond neighborly pleasantries), I would most likely have to contend with our downstairs neighbors. They were more suited to romantically pursuing the particular young ladies in our little penthouse. "I'm sure that they don't walk around half naked."

Myra smiled and leaned back in her chair and began swirling her wine. I began crushing the crust of my bread and sprinkling the flakes over my plate. Occasionally, one or two of them would, by chance, land on the table. "Anyway, I've heard there's an inherent danger in dating someone while living in the same building."

This brought an end to the swirling. Myra looked at her plate once more. She drained her glass and asked, "In the mood for dessert?"

I looked down at my plate. There sat the heap of uneaten food, covered in crusty debris. "Not particularly, no."

"Yeah," she said. "Neither am I."

We left the table, but the music ended before we could even finish cleaning up. I have to admit, I was relieved.

***

Friday morning, there was some tension, but we managed to be cordial to each other. Neither of us referred to the previous night's exchange. By the time I got back home, I felt little or no unease. Myra had apparently put the unpleasantness behind her as well. She offered to pick up a video for the both of us while I was having dinner. I understood the motivation behind her generosity, but I also knew that to turn down such a favor would provoke immediate wrath, rather than delaying, and perhaps totally evading, her anger. I've found that stretching Myra's anger out usually diminishes it as well.

I told her that I trusted her choice of movies, and I quickly ate a bland meal of partially reheated lasagna. Before she got back, I did both her dishes and mine, despite the fact that it was her turn to do the dishes. This would give me the leverage to balance out her graciousness. It was a particularly good night for such a favor, because we'd each had leftovers, which meant, of course, fewer dishes.

Myra returned with a romantic comedy. It started out mildly promising, but one-half to three-quarters of an hour into it, the music came on. It was quite loud. Some sort of techno/dance album with a throbbing beat. I looked over at Myra. "Do you want me to go talk to them now?"

She smiled back at me. "No. It's still early. Let them listen to it."

She took the remote and turned the volume several notches above what was really necessary. We finished watching the movie, rarely laughing now. Myra's initial lenience would no doubt factor into later negotiations with me. As the tape was rewinding, the music shut off, and we heard them trample down the stairs. There was a short pause and some yelling when they reached the bottom, and then the front door slammed. I looked at Myra. "Perhaps we'll have a quiet night tonight."

She patted my knee. "Maybe. But keep an ear open, just in case, okay?"

I agreed. The rest of the evening was pleasant enough. Around eleven o' clock, I announced that I was going off to bed.

"All right," Myra said. "But if you hear anything later, I want you to come check in with me."

Again, I agreed. I sat in bed, reading for a short time before turning off the lights. Predictably, the silence began to grate on me. My mind wandered aimlessly, keeping me awake. I almost wished for some tune to try naming. I watched the minutes tick by. Try as I might, I simply could not fall asleep.

Sometime around two-thirty (after bar time, I noted) they returned up the stairs. From my bedroom I could barely hear it, but I was quite certain that Myra was now awake. Within minutes, the music came on. I quickly turned on my side, so that my face was away from the bedroom door. Shortly thereafter, I heard Myra padding up to my room. I closed my eyes before I heard the hallway light click on. We each remained motionless for quite some time. After a half-hearted cough, I feigned waking and rolled over. There was Myra, in the doorway. She was wearing only her nightshirt, from what I could see.

At this point, I will confess to having envisioned certain scenarios in which Myra would show up to my room at night. I was not obsessed and maybe not even in love with her, but, when two theoretically compatible people live together, it's natural for either or both of them to consider such possibilities. Of course, none of my fantasies began with her wanting to discuss the volume of our neighbors' music, but her presence excited me a bit nonetheless.

"You hear it, right?"

I sat up and listened. "I hear it."

She took a few steps in. "Don't you think it's a bit loud?"

I sighed. Despite my intention to avoid taking a definite position, I couldn't argue the point. "It is a bit loud for this hour."

This concession brought Myra over to my bed. When she sat down, her night- shirt rode up a bit, exposing her legs even further. The combination of light from the hallway and darkness in my room presented me with a lovely silhouette. Her night shirt was a bit short, and it hung in a certain way, which gave a full display of her curvature, to use the mathematical term. This vision, combined with her proximity, set forth certain physical machinations throughout my body. Quite quickly, they began to find their inevitable outlet. Something as simple as a sigh and a slight forward tilt of the head (a move which brought a wave of soft, brown hair tumbling down, framing her face) sped the process along to undesirable results.

"So are you going to talk to them?"

I took a deep breath, hoping that relaxing might help to combat my body's inclinations. "Now?"

Myra stared at me for a moment. "Yes, now."

I sat up more and brought my knees to my chest, hoping that, if I could not combat my condition, I could at least hide it. "Give me a moment to wake up. I don't want to get up there and start speaking all in gobbledygook."

Myra grabbed my arm and shook it lightly. "Well hurry up. I want to get back to sleep."

Of course, her actions only exacerbated matters. I wasn't prepared to communicate with Myra the effects of her contact, so I
needed to maintain my ruse of a sleep-addled mind in order to
stage a delayed and graceful exit. I could only delay for so long,
though. "I should probably put some pants on."

This comment did not move Myra in the way I had hoped.
"Probably, unless you're trying to spend the night at their place."

Luckily, the darkness hid my face, which was doubtlessly crim-
son by this point. "Can you grab me a pair from the closet?"

"Does this mean you're awake enough to go?"

My annoyance with Myra was growing. Fortunately, as my
anger increased, my other feelings began to subside. "Just another
minute or two. Now may I please have my pants?"

She laughed and began to root through my closet. "Want some
cologne, too?"

"Just grab a pair from the basket." I clenched and unclenched
my fists, trying to work off the excitement Myra had brought me.
Trying to redistribute my blood.

"You don't want to put on your best for the ladies?" She had bent
over to search through my clothes. I quickly looked up at the ceiling and
began taking deep breaths. Luckily, the socks that might have had bodily
fluid stains were always carefully left in the bottom of the hamper.

"Get me my pants."

She tossed me a pair of slacks. As I reached for them, she said,
"Now don't tell them that I'm the one who told you to talk to them."

I brought the pants beneath my covers and struggled my way
into them, wriggling my legs like an incompetent swimmer. "But
you did."

"Why do I always have to be the bad guy?"

Pointing out that she actually was the bad guy (gender specific-
ities aside) would have gotten me nowhere. "I'll just tell them that
we thought the music was a bit loud."

"Not we." She plopped back onto the bed. By this point, I was
able to control myself much better. "Then they're going to think
that I'm the one who's doing all the complaining."

"Well..." I slid my legs out and pulled my pants tight to be sure
that there were no protrusions before I tried standing. I found I was
in the clear.

"So you don't think the music is loud?"

"Not to the point that I'd complain about it." I briefly contem-
plated confronting them shirtless, but my general physique lends
itself to neither intimidation nor admiration.

"Fine." She stood up. "Don't talk to them then. I'll just go back
to bed and try to sleep through it."

I quickly grabbed a plain t-shirt from the closet. "I'll go. Don't sulk."

I left the room and headed for the stairs before she had a chance
to reply. When I reached the door, I leaned in so that my ear was
almost touching it. I could not quite tell where they were in their
apartment. I was hoping that they were far enough away from the
door that I could knock lightly and tell Myra nobody answered.
I heard some rough shuffling, and I leaned in closer. It took me
a few seconds to realize that the shuffling was actually very near
the door. I was barely able to pull my head away before the door
opened. In the dim light of the stairway, I was not immediately
able to identify the man standing there. In fact, he recognized me
before I was able to place him. "Hey, man," he said.

At this point, I realized that it was one of my downstairs neighbors. I flattened my shirt out on my chest. "Hello, friend."

He smiled. "We keeping you up or are you just here to get in on the party?"

His pseudo-invitation, while not particularly inviting, was at least disarming. "I'm not much of a partier, thank you. As a matter of fact, I was up to ask about turning the music down a bit, if you wouldn't mind."

He held up his hands. "I'm all done here, Chief. You'll have to talk to one of them."

He then gave me a light pat on the shoulder and walked down the stairs. The door was still open, but he hadn't bothered to get either of the apartment's occupants. I stood at the door, peering into the room. From there, I was able to hear the music quite clearly, along with some small snatches of conversation.

"I'm surprised you didn't ask him to spend the night."

"Give him another week or two. I'm still scoping out that guy from my anthro class."

At this point, I began to notice that what I'd originally taken to be dim lighting was actually a haze. Apparently, they were smoking some substance or combination of substances. The clouds of smoke began to drift towards me. Their smell was not all together unpleasant.

"Another beer?"

"Sure."

With the door open, the shuffling was much clearer than it had been. It was approaching the door, but, assuming that their apartment was set up identically to ours, a trip to the refrigerator would not pass the door. There was a clinking of bottles, signifying that the refrigerator had indeed been reached.

As I stood in my reverie (perhaps the haze had already begun to affect me), I heard some movement from the landing beneath me. It was accompanied by a hiss. "Phillip."

I tensed and slowly turned. There, standing on the landing, was Myra, still in her nightshirt. "What's taking so long?"

There was a pause in the shuffling from the apartment.

"Phillip?" I looked back from Myra to the door. I tried waving her off, but I heard no movement to indicate that she'd returned to our apartment. One of the residents of the apartment came to the door. She was wearing a black mini-skirt and a tight, red top. Her eyes were huge and she didn't notice that her beers were foaming. It ran down the side of the bottles, over her hand, and onto the floor.

"Who the hell are you?"

"I'm downstairs."

She furrowed her brows. "What?"

"Your neighbor. Downstairs. I'm your downstairs neighbor."

She squinted at me. "You live with Paul?"

"Who?"

"Paul from downstairs."

"Oh. No, no. I'm from the second-floor apartment."

This seemed to ease her mind. She even began to notice the beer that she had was spilling over. "Shit," she said, and scurried back to her kitchen, dripping foam all over the floor. Lucky for her, our building had hardwoods.

I turned to Myra and renewed my efforts to wave her off. This time, I was able to get her to frown and walk away. Suddenly, the music stopped. This would help me immensely if I could just get back to Myra. When the occupants came back, they were each carrying a handful of paper towel and their partially empty beers. They got down on all fours and took turns wiping and drinking. The first roommate, the blonde girl with the mini-skirt and red top, said, "What do you want?"

"Actually, I only came up here to see if you would turn your music down a tad, but, since you've shut it off, it really shouldn't be a problem. Have a good night."

I began to turn, hoping that their inebriation would prevent them from pursuing the point any further. Unfortunately, the first girl said, "Hey. Did you just open our door without knocking?"

"No. Your friend left it open."

The second girl, a slightly healthier-looking woman with light brown hair (not unlike Myra's), looked at the first and frowned. "Paul just left our door open?"

"Paul from downstairs?" I asked.

The first girl shook her head. "He must have been way more wasted than he was showing."

I knew that, eventually, Paul would relate to them what had happened, so I said, "Actually, I was here when he left. I'm sure that's why he left the door open."

This led to an exchange of glances between my neighbors. "Paul left like five minutes ago. Have you been standing at our door that whole time?"

I began to slowly back down the stairs. "He and I spoke for a bit, and then Myra heard us chatting, so she came out and she had some things to say to me. Then you were already at the door, so..."

The second girl spoke. "Some things to say, huh?"

I had made my way about three steps down by now. "Myra likes her input to be known."

The girls snickered. "So we've noticed."

While I was tempted to join in the laughter, I couldn't be sure that Myra was not listening by our door. "Oh, she's a fine person. She just keeps a clear interest in her surroundings."

The girls laughed again. I was now hoping that Myra was sitting in her room, out of earshot. "Really, she just gets agitated when she doesn't get her sleep. But, then, we all do."

The second girl said, "We'll try to keep the noise down."

I thanked them and wished them a good night. Each of them replied in kind and then the door closed. As, I tiptoed down to my own apartment, I heard no sound from inside. When I opened the door, Myra was standing in the center of our living room. Her expression was hard to read, especially because she'd left the lights off. "They're turning it off for the night."

"What did they say?"

I closed the door and turned the lock. "Nothing. Sorry for our troubles. Won't happen again. That sort of thing."

"And you believe them?"

I turned, but still didn't make eye contact with Myra. "I didn't want to accuse them of lying. They turned the music off for tonight. What else do you want?"

She sighed. I looked into her eyes. They looked dark and full. "I did my best."

She hugged me and said. "I know. I'm not really mad at you."

I returned her embrace. Her hair smelled softly sweet. Just the tiniest hint of the morning's shampoo with a soft undercurrent of sweat from her day. A few strands even brushed against my cheek.

She was the first to break our hug, after which she wished me a good night with a kiss on the cheek and then went to bed. I stood in the living room for a bit, listening to the quiet. Shortly thereafter, I heard soft snores coming from Myra's room. There was no sound from above. I went back to my own bed and lay down, still in my clothes. Even in my room, I could have sworn that I heard Myra's snores. I stared at the ceiling, not even able to shut my eyes, just listening for the music to come back on and thinking my night away.

The Law of Entropy

Ralph thought the band had gone into rehearsal with the best of intentions. At some point, they'd agreed to come up with some more material and get a little more used to each other so that they could sound like a band playing together instead of three guys soloing and one guy singing. Rehearsal had even started off pretty well. While the rest of the band was setting up, Perry came down the stairs in a skirt and a tanktop, carrying a case of beer, but he was wearing boxers underneath the skirt, which was cool of him. After two sessions of accidentally seeing Perry's ass every few minutes, Andy and Tim had told Perry that he had to start sporting some underwear on nights he was wearing a skirt. Perry said it was a comfort and movement thing, but he thought boxers would be okay. Tim had told Ralph that Perry was doing it to make it easier for him to get head onstage, but Ralph couldn't tell if Tim was just screwing with him. Ralph didn't really care that much about Perry's skirt, since he never looked far enough away from his guitar to see Perry's ass one way or the other, but he appreciated Perry cooperating.

They got through the one full song they had, and it was all right. Although it wasn't really their song. It was a cover of "My

Generation" with alternate lyrics about crack and pissing on public property. Mostly about crack, though. The band tried a lot of covers; they only had a few bits of original songs. A lot of the time, they'd just start in on some lyrics Perry had and hope that inspiration would come in the middle of playing. That's how the song Ralph was playing had started. Unfortunately, by the time Perry got to the chorus for the first time, the law of entropy had taken over and things went to shit like always.

But Ralph was still trying to play and move a little. Ralph couldn't look away while playing, but he could stumble around so that it looked like he was drunk and not just a hack. They all needed some practicing before they could tour, but Perry was tight with some club owners in the greater Madison area. He'd get some shows booked, and that would put the Dry Humps on the right track. But Ralph worried. He wasn't sure that the other guys had put that much thought into the band. The only plan they'd ever talked about was to stay small until the Dead Milkmen reunited. But now that their bass player had died, Ralph didn't know what the Dry Humps would do.

For now, Ralph was trying. He tried making his way over to the second mic stand, to put in an "ooo-ah," or a couple of "yeah's." Instead, he tripped over something, and he almost cracked his head against the concrete floor of the basement.

"Aah," Ralph said after catching himself with his right hand. "My playing hand."

Ralph stood up and shook his hand out while the music died away. It hurt a little, but it didn't seem broken or sprained or anything. After Ralph checked his hand, he noticed that it was Perry that he'd tripped over. Perry was lying on the ground and laughing a little.

"It's not funny," Ralph said to Perry. "If I hurt my playing hand, then all the progress I've made could have been shot to hell."

Andy, the bass player, tossed his beer against the basement wall. "Damn it, Perry, Ralph is right. We might have to put off touring."

Ralph looked at Andy, but didn't say a word. He just shook his head and started packing up his guitar.

Perry started to get up. "Aw, come on, man. We're sorry."

Ralph closed his eyes. "Can we just get through an entire song that somebody else didn't write? I mean, that's actually our own song?"

Perry could drive Ralph nuts. He had so much talent, and he just pissed it away drinking with Tim and Andy.

"Yeah, well," Perry said, "I'm just waiting for Tim."

Ralph stopped packing up his guitar and looked over at the drum set. The stool was empty. "Yeah, where did Tim go?"

Nobody answered. Andy went over to the beer he'd thrown against the wall. As Andy stood up, he shook the can back and forth. There must have been some left, because he brought the can up to his mouth and tipped his head back.

***

Perry had the ability to really electrify a crowd. Ralph had seen it first hand. A few years back, when he was still in high school, Ralph had gone to see a show at O'Cayz. It's where the hardcore bands played. Ralph couldn't remember who the headliners had been, he only remembered The One-Trick Ponies. That was the band Perry sang for at the time. He got a couple of girls from the audience to come up onstage and dance. Ralph had been mesmerized.

After the show, he had gone up to Perry, who was at the bar, talking to one of the girls who had danced. Ralph stood next to him for about ten minutes before Perry finally looked over and said, "Hey."

Ralph nodded. "Great show."

"Thanks."

Ralph had watched Perry drink for a little bit, and then asked, "Do you have any tapes or CD's for sale?"

Perry lit a cigarette and looked at Ralph. "No, but give our drummer your address and we can hook you up with our fan club letter. It's called the Pony Express."

Ralph smiled. "Okay."

As Ralph had started to turn away to track down the One-Trick's drummer, Perry put his hand on Ralph's arm. "Hey, kid. We don't really have a fan club. I was just kind of fucking with you. You know, Pony Express."

Ralph started mumbling and smiling. As he talked, even he wasn't really paying attention to what he was saying. He just let his words go. Perry patted him on the arm and smiled.

Ralph had laughed. Luckily, it had been too dark for anyone to see him blushing. After some more mumbling and laughing, Perry had agreed to stay in touch with Ralph on MySpace back when people actually used it. In the months after that show, Ralph had been to a couple of parties at Perry's place. One time, he'd been trying to impress some of them, so he started talking about stuff from the college courses he was taking. He was only going part time. He told this one girl about the law of entropy. How every-thing just keeps getting more and more fucked up, more "chaotic" his teacher had said. Though the teacher also said that chaotic was more like everything being the same than it was an explosion or anarchy or something. That's how the universe ran. The girl said that he sounded deep while he was telling her about it, but she still didn't make out with him.

***

After stomping through the hallway between the basement and the bathroom twice, Ralph went into Perry's bedroom. There was Tim, shirtless, sitting on Perry's bed and leaning over a copy of Barely Legal, from Perry's porn collection. Ralph couldn't tell if Tim was ignoring him or if he couldn't see Ralph at first, because Tim's hair was hanging over his face.

Ralph waited for Tim to acknowledge him somehow. After about half a minute, Tim looked up at Ralph and held up the magazine. On the back was an ad for phone-sex lines. "Hey, you want one?"

"I want a decent drummer."

Tim tossed the magazine to the foot of Perry's bed. A couple of pages flipped back so that the table of contents was showing. "You look pretty tense there, Ralph. You sure you don't want one of the magazines? Perry's got a pretty sweet one from March a couple years ago."

Ralph did want one of the magazines. In fact, he wanted one pretty badly, but he wanted the band to get better a little more than he wanted a magazine. "Come on," he said. "Why don't you just come downstairs and practice some more?"

Tim went over to Perry's bedroom closet and got another magazine. "I'll start practicing seriously when we get some songs. Real songs."

Ralph looked at the floor. He'd tried writing songs, but every time he started one, it ended up being about some girl he'd never got up the balls to ask out. Usually the check-out girl from Sunrise. "Why don't you guys write some? You've all been playing for a lot longer than I have, and Andy and Perry are both older than us." Tim shrugged, got back onto Perry's bed, and opened up the magazine he'd just grabbed. "I don't know. Talk to Perry, I guess. He's our mealticket."

Ralph nodded. That was almost true. There was no reason why it shouldn't be true. Tim was just looking at the new magazine that could've been anything. Ralph turned away from him and went downstairs. The basement looked dark after being in Perry's room. Perry was leaning against the wall, next to an old couch he kept downstairs. Andy was telling him a story, and Ralph could tell that it was about Tank Abbot. "Yeah, he actually got suspended from UFC. I mean, he gets paid to hurt people, and he's too violent for that? That's messed up."

Perry was shaking his head. "Yeah, I know, but we can't use his name for a band, man. We're gonna be the Dry Humps. If we call ourselves Tank Abbot, we're gonna draw such a hardcore crowd. It just wouldn't go with our original vision of a band that would tour with the Dead Milkmen, you know?"

Andy shrugged. "I know. I'm just saying it's pretty intense, that's all. It would be a good name for somebody; not us necessarily."

Perry closed his eyes and nodded. "Maybe write a song about it or something. We could use another song. But if we ever put it out, your name goes on it. I don't want Tank Abbot busting into my house, and breaking my legs or something because he hears I'm singing about him without his permission."

They stood quietly for a second and then looked over at Ralph. "What's up, Chief?" Perry asked.

"Tim and I think we should take the rest of the night off. Maybe we can get together again tomorrow night?"

Perry grimaced. "I gotta work tomorrow night."

Ralph looked down. "Oh."

Perry said, "Maybe the rest of you guys can get together for a few beers and try to think up some songs or something. Andy's got an idea for a song about Tank Abbot, right, man?"

Andy shrugged and went to pack up his bass. "Okay if I leave this here tonight?"

"Long as you don't mind the roaches using it while you're gone."

Andy nodded and turned to Ralph. "Do we know where we're meeting tomorrow?"

Ralph shrugged. "I'll give you and Tim a call."

Andy gave Ralph a thumbs up and left. Perry plopped down on the couch. Ralph looked at him, then around at the basement. There were a couple of old cardboard boxes against the wall opposite the stairway and a faded Ramones poster sitting behind Tim's drum set. Perry kept the couch and a cooler by the stairs. Other than that, it was pretty much all band equipment. Ralph wondered if it looked any different when the One Tricks had played there. "Man, we've really gotta get everyone on the same page."

"Long way to go," Perry said.

Ralph moved closer to the couch, but didn't sit down. "Perry, do you think we'll ever be any good?"

Perry smiled. "Hey, we're a punk band. We're not supposed to be good. Just a bunch of noise, right?"

Ralph smiled and nodded. He waited a few seconds and then tried again. "No, really though. I mean, do you think we'll do anything?"

Perry shook his head. "Man, nobody ever does anything."

Ralph blinked a few times. "What do you mean?"

"Nothing. You need a ride home?"

"If it's cool, I'll take one." Ralph knew that Perry had been drinking, but if Perry offered a ride, Ralph trusted him to be okay.

"Sure," said Perry. "Just let me get something else on."

Ralph finished putting some of the equipment away while Perry was upstairs. After he got things to the point where they were only as disorganized as usual, Ralph went upstairs, carrying his guitar with him. Perry was in the living room with Tim, watching TV. One of those animal shows. A couple of lions were wrestling in some mating ritual. Ralph watched it for about five minutes before Perry looked over at him. "Hey man, ready?" Ralph nodded and then waved to Tim, who didn't seem to notice. Perry was in cut-off jean shorts and a black tank top. Ralph watched Perry light up a cigarette as he tossed his guitar in the back of Perry's truck. Perry had a body that let him wear tank tops. Ralph was wearing a long-sleeve shirt and camo pants.

There was a McDonald's bag on the floor of the passenger's side of Perry's truck. Ralph pushed it towards the seat as he got in. Perry was sitting in the driver's seat, fumbling through a box of tapes. He didn't seem to be finding whatever he was looking for. "Man, I bet Andy still has it."

Ralph watched, not asking what it was that Perry was looking for. Perry grumbled something to himself and put in a Black Flag tape. Ralph couldn't tell which one it was, but it was definitely after Henry Rollins took over as lead singer. Perry backed the truck up.

"So, Ralphy Boy, you doing okay?"

Ralph smiled at the dashboard. He liked it when Perry called him Ralphy Boy. "Yeah, hanging in there, I guess."

Perry took the cigarette out of his mouth for a bit. "You know, if you ever need to just talk, any of us are there for you, man."

Ralph looked over at Perry. Perry was watching the road. He had dark pockets under his eyes and his hair was as messed up as hair that short could be, but he still looked cool. "How come you never tried to get a real band together?"

Perry laughed. "Hey, you saying the Dry Humps aren't a real band?"

Ralph laughed too. After a little bit, he said, "No, really. You know what I mean."

Perry took a long drag off his cigarette. "Lots of ways of looking at whether a band is good or not. This one seems good enough to me. Maybe not performance wise, but for what I'm looking for we're fine. It's there. I mean, someday, we might be able to do some shows, maybe even go on a tour of a few cities. Probably not, but hell, if we don't, so what? We're no worse off than we are right now."

Ralph thought that was bad enough. He sighed, but didn't say anything. The rest of the ride home was mostly quiet. Ralph didn't feel like talking that much. Even to Perry. Instead, he just looked out the windshield. On the clear night's sky, he was seeing his check-out girl from Sunrise Foods. If Ralph saw her when he walked into the store, he'd change his shopping list. Buy more vegetables and less cookies. Once, he even bought a heavy-metal maga-zine. When she ran it over the register, he said, "I'm in a band." "Yeah?" she'd said, not making eye contact. That night, her hair was up in a bun and she wasn't wearing any earrings. Ralph still thought she looked beautiful. He wanted to tell her how beautiful she was. "Yep," said Ralph. "I play guitar."

"Your band play anywhere?" She checked out the celery that Ralph would end up mostly throwing away.

"Just in my friend's basement right now. We kind of just started. But maybe if we play somewhere, I'll let you know."

The girl looked Ralph in the eyes and, for a second, he lost his breath. Then she said, "That'll be 52.67."

Ralph had to pay with credit.

***

"Want some help taking your guitar up?"

The truck was parked right out front of Ralph's apartment building. Ralph shook his head. He hadn't even really noticed that they were there. "No thanks, but thanks for the ride, though."

Ralph started to get out, but Perry stopped him, saying, "Hey, don't be afraid to bring a song in sometime. I know you said some-thing before about working on one or something, and God knows we could use one. You don't even have to finish it, really, just bring in whatever you have, and we'll figure out the music as we go."

Ralph tried to smile, but he just felt drained for some reason.

80

Perry nodded at him, and Ralph got out of the truck. The air felt cool, and that felt good under his heavy clothes. The weather had been all over the place lately. As soon as you got used to the heat, it would cool off, and when it was cool long enough to be used to it, it would heat up. Ralph felt like he could never catch a break. He grabbed his guitar from the back of Perry's truck and went to the building's door. He leaned the guitar against the wall and started to go for his keys. As Ralph was opening the front door, the guitar started sliding to the ground. He dropped his keys and caught the case. He tried to brush the keys over to his hands with his foot, but he just ended up stumbling a little. Eventually, he just let the guitar case slowly slide down to the ground and picked up the keys so that he could open the door partway. Then, Ralph reached for the guitar case and slid his foot in the door. After some rummaging, he was able to slide the guitar inside. His face was burning and he'd even started sweating a little. He looked up, and Perry was still there in his truck. Perry waved to Ralph. Ralph smiled and waved back. He crawled in the door and watched Perry back up and leave. Ralph nodded. He'd write a song for the Dry Humps.

***

A week or so later, the Dry Humps were at it again. Not much had come out of the brainstorming session with Tim and Andy other than an agreement that Perry's girlfriend from two relationships ago had been the hottest any of them had seen. Ralph had never met her.

Eventually, the jam died down. Perry went over to the cooler to get some beers. Ralph went to his guitar case to get his new song while Andy told Tim about the time a referee had to pull Tank Abbot off a guy who was definitely beyond consciousness, let alone in a fighting state. Ralph smoothed out the crumpled piece of paper on his leg.

Perry gave a beer each to Andy and Tim. Ralph drank only at parties, although it had been a while since Perry had thrown one. "What've you got there, Ralphy Boy?"

Ralph looked at each of the Dry Humps. "I think we should do this song."

Perry smiled at him. "Let's have a look."

Ralph handed him the song and waited as Perry and the rest of the Dry Humps squinted at the paper in the dim light of the basement. The chorus was:

You see the prices, but you don't see me
  it leaves me filled with such doubt
Oh Check-out Girl, why the fuck
  won't you just check me out!

After a minute or so, the band started laughing. Tim said, "Dude, this is hilarious."

Andy said, "Yeah, we could even do two versions. Like, a whiny, bitchy one, and then a loud version."

Perry shook his head. "No, no man. Just one version, but the first part is whiny, and then the chorus is loud. Right, Ralphy?"

Ralph was furrowing his brows. He was glad the band liked it, but it seemed like they weren't getting it. "Um."

After a little, Perry said, "It's good, man. It's funny."

"Yeah," Andy said. "It's like a love song that Tank Abbot would write."

Perry shot Andy a glance, and Andy was quiet. Then Perry looked back at Ralph. "Hey, don't worry man. We're definitely doing the song. It'll be awesome."

Tim started laughing. "You know what it's like? It's really like 'Institutionalized.' You know, when he's sitting there and asking his mom for a Pepsi, and he's going nuts, just because she won't give him a Pepsi. And it's like he thinks a Pepsi is gonna make him feel all better or something."

Three out of the four Dry Humps started laughing. Ralph just smiled. He didn't want to screw up how good they all thought the song was. Law of fucking entropy and all. He looked at Perry, and Perry said, "See man. It's good."

Ralph nodded. "Thanks. Look, why don't you guys talk about the music to go with it or something. I gotta go drain the snake."

The other Dry Humps smiled. "Yeah," Perry said. "Cool."

Ralph went up the stairs a lot lighter than usual. He wasn't sure if his feet even made any noise; his heart was thumping too loud for him to hear. After going to the bathroom, Ralph took some Kleenex and went into Perry's room. He started looking through Perry's porn collection. Finally, he was one of the guys. A Dry Hump.

Toast

About half an hour before what would be a record-setting performance, Mitch was still sitting in his tent trying to focus. He was tapping his fingers on Rhonda's metal frame when the thrower that the festival folks assigned him came in to meet him. The thrower was a big, bulky guy with a silver stud through his bottom lip, a silver earring in each ear, and a metal ring through his septum. "So you're the toaster guy, huh?" asked the thrower.

"Yup."

The thrower grunted and told Mitch that he had thirty minutes until showtime. Mitch saw him looking at the ankle brace and shaking his head. A few people had that today. Mitch thanked the man for the time check, and he put on his Walkman. The tape was of Tony Robbins, that tall motivational speaker. Tony made perfect sense to Mitch. The main thing Tony kept talking about was that everyone was motivated to seek pleasure and avoid pain. Tony's ideas seemed good. Almost obvious.

Mitch closed his eyes. As clear as the basics of Tony's plan were, the humidity and nerves made it hard for Mitch to follow the details, like how he was supposed to use the ideas. Mitch could only catch snatches, even though he'd heard the tape a few times before.

He opened his eyes and looked over at Rhonda, who, despite her missing nub, was still more supportive than Nina was. He touched her once, on the sticker, and watched Rhonda wobble slightly.

She got her wobble the same night she got her stickers. Or the other way around, maybe. Nina had sawed off one of Rhonda's nubs one night while Mitch was out trying to clear his head after a fight they'd had. Nina had left Rhonda, the bread knife she'd used on her, and a note saying, "Now she's a cripple, just like you. Love, Nina." The note had been written in lipstick; it looked like a little kid had written it with a big, red crayon. Nina could act like a little kid a lot.

When Mitch had seen it, he'd turned around and left without a word. He went for a long drive. Later that night, he'd come home with the sheet of stickers with smiling yellow bears. Each of their stomachs had "Grin and Bear It" written on it. He took one sticker off, then folded up the sheet and put it into his wallet. The single sticker went on Rhonda's side. After putting it on, he'd patted Rhonda and put a couple of pieces of bread in her to make a sandwich. She'd said, "Toast down," in her normal voice, professional, but kind of sweet, too. That was the moment he knew he'd perform at the festival. Rhonda and Mitch were both just household objects to Nina, now that she was drinking again.

***

Mitch could remember the night he'd heard about the festival. Nina had been wearing a blue sequined dress with a cut up the left side. It was cut so that it was loose around her legs, easily letting her walk all around the dark, shiny stage, but tight enough to hug her ass. She'd stalk from side to side, stopping only to either wrap her leg around a pole or trade a kiss for some money from one of the audience members. Mitch wished he could be on stage with Nina, but the brace kept him from moving like her, and he probably wasn't good looking enough to be a drag queen, anyway. So, Mitch just sat in the back with some of the older guys who came to the bar.

"I'm feeling like a beer," Mitch said to the old timer sitting next to him, still watching Nina. "Want one?"

The old man was quiet, but Mitch knew he'd drink one if it was put in front of him. While Mitch was getting the beers, the old man was fumbling around in his jacket pockets. He pulled out some fliers and a little catalog. "I ever tell you about Valhalla, Mitch?"

Mitch pushed an extra dollar over the bar and nodded to the bartender. "You mean like with Thor or whatever?"

The old man squinted. "Huh?"

"Like the..." Mitch handed him the beer. "Never mind. What is it?"

The old man sipped his beer. "Festival. You might get a kick out of it."

The old guy pushed one of the fliers over to Mitch. A cheap little thing with the history of some festival, the Valhalla festival, it said. After the history, there were a few vague descriptions from people Mitch had never heard of. When Mitch looked up from the pamphlet, he saw that the old man had slid the catalog in front of him. It had all sorts of oddities. There were motor oil t-shirts (in honor of Christopher Stevens, the Valhalla Record Book's first entry), little Thor hammers that said "Get Hammered at the Fest!" and porn magazines. The faces of the models in them were covered up by cut-out pictures of serial killers' faces. They showed one of the pictures; it was of a very young girl, who apparently was a natural redhead, sitting on a kitchen counter. Her knees were spread wide, but her ankles were held close together by the green panties she wore around them. Her hands were touching her inner thighs. In place of her head, someone had put a shot of John Wayne Gacy's. In the picture they'd used, Gacy had been wearing clown makeup and a rainbow wig. The caption said that the girl's turn-on's were walks on the beach, juggling, and murder. Her hobbies included lurking, cheerleading, stamp collecting, and death.

Mitch laughed and shook his head, flipping through the catalog instead of watching Nina. There was a plain, white t-shirt with brick red letters that said, "Flipper Babies Welcome."

"What's this?" he asked.

The old man leaned over just a bit and gave a short breath out of his nose. "Flipper babies. Festival's mascot."

Mitch nodded and took another drink. "They have flipper babies at the festival?"

The old man frowned. "Aren't any flipper babies anymore. Too much science. Or not enough science, maybe."

Mitch kept the flier to talk to Nina about going. The old man nodded and drained the rest of his beer.

A few days later, Mitch left the flier near the toaster, the one they had before Rhonda. While he and Nina were having breakfast, she picked it up. "What is this?"

"One of the regulars at the club gave it to me. That old guy who sits in the back.

I thought it looked kind of cool." Mitch took a spoonful of cereal.

Nina held the flier between her thumbs and pointing fingers while she waited for her English muffin to toast in the speechless toaster, the one they had before Rhonda. "Mitch, these people look like a bunch of weirdos."

Slowly, Mitch got up and started hobbling towards the fridge. As he passed behind Nina, he said, "All part of the show."

Nina picked up the butter knife and pointed it at Mitch. "Show? These kind of people have serious problems."

"They're dedicated." Mitch grabbed the orange juice. "The very first guy, Christopher Stevens, he put down eight ounces of motor oil. Can you imagine?"

"Fantastic." Nina tossed the pamphlet on the counter.

Mitch set the orange juice on the counter for Nina and headed back to the table. "Read it. They were betting about whether some actor really drank oil in Over the Top. You know, the arm-wrestling movie with Stallone."

"That's supposed to impress me?"

"You like Stallone, honey. You think he's hot."

Nina's English muffin popped up. "Yeah, well they're not Stallone. They're a bunch of freaks and idiots."

Mitch shook his head. "They're entertainers. Like you."

Nina turned around and looked at him. She didn't say a word, but she kept looking at him. Mitch shrank and dragged his bad ankle behind the rest of his body. "I didn't...I just meant you're both entertaining. That's all. I mean, you're both entertaining, but, like, in totally different ways. Look, Nina, I'm sorry."

Nina grabbed her English muffin. She waited a few seconds

before smearing margarine on it. The only sounds were the scraping of the knife across the toasted muffin and Mitch's left foot
dragging across the floor. Mitch ate his breakfast on the couch in
the living room, and they didn't speak most of the rest of the day.

***

Mitch looked down at his brace. While Tony Robbins talked about
how to set good goals, Mitch clanked it on one of the legs of his
chair and sighed. He wished Nina would have been more into the
festival. Maybe she could have even been a performer there. Last
year's festival had seemed great to Mitch. There was too much
to see, if anything. There were the record setters, like the giant
who got into the books for most vomit expelled from a human
body in five minutes (3.7 liters), and the sideshows, too. One of
the sideshows was a two-stage performance concept. On the front
stage, there was a performance artist with raw bacon stapled to
her crotch, and on the second stage, a group of mentally retarded
people (the Short-Bus Choir, the emcee called them) would imitate
her. From the moment she got out onto the stage, she was yelling at
the choir to step back. After dancing around the stage in a pretend
stripshow for a little bit, the artist pulled a vibrator out of a holster
hanging from the slit in her skirt and started to roll the vibrator in
the meat. One of the members of the choir unzipped his pants
and started to play with himself. The performance artist walked
off the stage and told the audience to fuck off. The crowd just
hooted and laughed.

Mitch was disappointed when the choir member stuffed his dick
back into his pants without coming. It was kind of sad. Nina lit up

89

a cigarette. "I think the whole thing is disgusting. It's not funny to laugh at those people."

Mitch wasn't sure if Nina was talking about the choir or the performance artist. He nodded and shuffled off to a stage where someone was eating a plate of tumor that had been removed from one of his arms. In order to keep the tumor in an edible state, the man had apparently had to go to a shady doctor. The scars on his arms were terrible. Mitch wanted to get a little closer to the action, but Nina refused to help him get through the crowd to the stage. Just another way for her to be negative. She'd been that way even after agreeing to take Mitch to the festival.

***

When Mitch had first brought Rhonda home, after the trouble started, Nina had been waiting for him. There was a bottle (still in the brown bag it must've come in) on the floor by her feet. As Mitch shuffled in with the box, Nina rubbed her nose and frowned. "What's that?"

"A toaster."

"We already have a toaster."

"This one talks." Mitch plopped the box down on the floor and started to open it

"Jesus Christ, Mitch. I can't believe you'd waste our money on something so stupid. I don't know if you just didn't get it or what, but this break I'm on isn't a paid vacation for me."

"So get a job."

"I have a job, you prick."

Mitch took his new toaster, Rhonda, out of her box and started

90

to pop off the styrofoam casing around her. "I just wanted a toaster to keep me company. It's cheaper than a pet. Or a kid."

"Prick."

Nina kept yelling at Mitch, egging him on. While she was yelling at him, he took a deep breath and envisioned himself just like his new toaster. Warm on the inside, but encased in durable metal, like his ankle brace. Rhonda could take a cold, dry pop tart and make it hot and tender. Eventually, Nina's tirade died down, and she went into her room. Mitch had started thinking of it as being "her room" and not "their room" for a couple of weeks now. Mitch unclenched his jaw and sighed. He'd really wanted a beer.

Sometimes the attacks got physical. Mitch could take getting hit with magazines or smaller kitchen utensils, but what really got him was when she first kicked his ankle. Nina had found that little bit of space between where his brace protected his foot and where it clamped onto his shin. It was terrible, going down. He had to crawl into a corner and turn his back to Nina. Once he was down, he could easily handle Nina's abuse; it was the going down that got to him. The flash of pain and the uncontrollable crumpling. It was too much. His ankle ached all day and through the night.

The next day, while Nina was passed out on the couch, Mitch took off Rhonda's shell. He saw the heating coils inside. After staring at Rhonda's interior for a while, he twanged one of the coils lightly, and then he put the face back on. There wasn't much give to the coil, so the twang wasn't very loud. Just a light, clicky reverberation. Once Rhonda was back together, Mitch took a deep breath and put in a pop tart. While he was eating it, Nina came into the kitchen. He looked at her but didn't say anything.

"Finally figure out how to get head from that thing?"

Mitch sat down on the floor and finished his pop tart. He could feel Nina watching him the whole time.

***

Mitch looked around his tent. Nobody was near. He was surprised that, for how lousy security was, more people didn't bother the performers. It even surprised him a little that he hadn't tried to talk to one of the performers last year. Not that Nina would have gone for it, pissed as she was.

He'd tried smoothing things over. Giving her peace offerings. Flowers, perfume, a new feather boa. None of it seemed to make up, although the boa finally at least got a roll of the eyes. Nina took it into their bedroom and came out a few minutes later. Mitch was sitting at the kitchen table, fiddling with a matchbook. Nina leaned against the hallway doorframe, the boa draped over her shoulders. Mitch looked up, trying to keep his expression as blank as possible. Eventually, she sighed and gave a tired-looking smile. "If it's really that big to you, we can go to the festival this summer."

Mitch smiled at her. "Thanks."

As Nina turned and started to walk away, Mitch said, "Nina."

She stopped but didn't turn back around. Mitch started to lift himself up to go to her, but, about halfway to standing, Nina held up a hand. Mitch stopped. "Just leave it at thanks, Mitch."

With that, Nina flipped the boa over her shoulder and went back to the bedroom, leaving Mitch propped up on the back of a chair and the table.

Later, after they'd spent a day at the festival, Mitch tried apologizing again. While they were lying in the saggy hotel bed in the spoon position, which always impressed Mitch, because he never felt Nina's real sex, Nina said, "Mitch?"

"Yeah?"

"Do you really think I'm like them? Like those freaks?"

Mitch propped himself up on his left elbow, trying to get a better view of her face. Between the festival and the sex, he was feeling generous. "Honey, I didn't mean it like that. I just meant that they're performers, like you. Not like you, I mean, I would never want to date any of the people who go for records there. Just...they're up onstage, you're up onstage."

Nina sniffled. "You don't take what I do very seriously, do you?"

Mitch didn't know what to say. Nina got paid to wander around a stage in drag. "Sweetheart, I didn't even mean it, to be honest. It's just something I said to get you to go with me to the festival."

Nina didn't say anything.

"I'm sorry."

Still nothing.

Softer, "I love you."

After a couple of minutes of silence, Mitch rolled away. It was hard for the two of them to sleep in the little motel bed without touching, but they did it. Sometimes, Mitch thought they didn't even breathe, except for small sighs and shakes.

***

As the first side of the motivational tape was ending, a festival worker told Mitch that it was time to go. Mitch nodded and followed the worker onto the stage. An emcee with a Lone-Ranger mask, stockings, and a large strap-on dildo, was doing a so-so job of pumping up the crowd for Mitch's record. Mostly, he was explaining to them that Mitch had a physical shortcoming that made his ankle brace necessary, and that it wasn't cheating in any way. Mitch thought that the emcee was a dink.

The emcee then gave a quick idea of what it was Mitch was trying. How many toasters could he get hit in the head or face with before falling down? There were a few claps as Mitch came up the right side of the stage and the thrower came up the left. The thrower picked up the first toaster by its slots, spun his arm in a full circle, and let it go. Mitch scrunched up his face and looked at the ground. The toaster smashed against the top of his head. Luckily, the flat bottom had hit him. Still, he took a step back with his right foot (the good one), and the crowd gasped. Rather than falling, though, Mitch righted himself, like an Olympic gymnast after a rough dismount. Most of the crowd clapped and yelled, but a couple of them up front said, "His brace is strapped to the stage."

Mitch took a deep breath and muttered to himself, "Toast down."

Then, he looked at the thrower and nodded. The thrower tossed a second toaster, this time in more of an arc than a straight shot, but it still hurt. Again, Mitch stumbled, but he didn't fall. After number five, Mitch's head was bleeding pretty well. The thrower looked around and eventually looked back at Mitch, who nodded and said, "Toast down!" out loud.

The crowd must have misunderstood, because they laughed and started chanting, "Touchdown, touchdown." Except for a couple of kids up front who said that Mitch had just admitted that his brace was bolted down to the stage. Mitch gritted his teeth and nodded at the thrower.

The thrower threw the next toaster by the cord, spinning it around a few times before letting it go. He ended up missing Mitch all together. The crowd booed him for that, so he went back to gripping the toasters by the slots.

After fourteen toasters, Mitch was reeling. He tried to mumble his mantra, but he knew that his time was up. He bit down hard on his back teeth, and said, "This one's for you, Rhonda."

The edge cracked hard against Mitch's left temple. He lurched back and then bent forward at the waist. The crowd gasped. Mitch righted himself, and they went crazy. He held up his hand and nodded to the crowd. Most of the crowd kept clapping for quite awhile. Even the thrower joined in. They were still clapping when Mitch fell to the stage.

When he came to, he was at the first aid tent. A man with a cigarette in his mouth and sandals on his feet was stitching Mitch up. A few of the people from the crowd followed him over to tell him how awesome he was. Mitch smiled and thanked them. They talked for a few minutes about how Mitch came up with the idea to take on toasters. He just shrugged. "Got pissed that I couldn't fit my bagels in, I guess."

The group laughed at that. When the smoker with the sandals was done stitching, he told Mitch to drink some orange juice or soda before walking around. Somebody handed Mitch a "Flipper Babies" t-shirt, and everyone went off to see other records. Mitch sat on the ground for a few minutes, looking at his new shirt. He used it to dab up some of the blood that nobody had bothered to wipe off his face. He knew that it would stain the shirt, but that was all right because of where it came from.

Mitch picked up Rhonda and headed off to the nearest beer garden. A worker there looked at Rhonda and then back at Mitch. "How can you be hugging a toaster after all that? It must've hurt like hell."

Mitch understood why the woman might think that, but she obviously didn't understand that Rhonda was different from the other toasters. Special. Mitch just chuckled and shrugged. He set Rhonda down and tapped one of the "Grin and Bear It" stickers on the side. The woman shook her head and handed Mitch a plastic cup of beer. "On the house," she said.

Mitch smiled at her. "Thanks," he said. "That's sweet of you."

Displays

My wife is pointing out a big Santa in a chimney on the left. "Watch" she says. Then, to our daughter Kaley, "There he goes". It's one of those inflatable deals where the chimney and the Santa are both big balloons. Animatronic, I guess, because, sure enough, down the chimney the thing goes. It looks big, cartoonish. Kaley giggles. She and my wife are enjoying themselves in the backseat. My son is hard to read. I look from the yard with the balloon Santa to the house itself. The curtains are drawn, which doesn't mean anything automatically, but it's not something to gloss over, either. I pull over and say, "Let's see if he'll come out again." Kaley's excited, but Jimmy, who's edging closer to teenage years, is playing with his Gameboy knockoff. I'm preparing myself for the fact that he and I will come to be opponents in a very short time. It's the sort of thing that you can't really believe will happen, but that you eventually go through. I assume you, do, anyway. It's hard to remember how things like that went with my parents, and I don't know if asking would even help that much. Getting it comes too late. That's a lot of what parenting is, of course.

"He's coming up," Kaley says. My wife, Liz, says, "I see him." I look in the rearview mirror and say, "You see him, Jimmy?" He says, "Yeah" without looking up. I don't say anything, and I don't know if that's the right thing or not. I look at this house's garage. Doors for two cars and plenty of extra room in between the two doors. It doesn't look like there's real security, either. The husband might have nice tools, and it might be easy to get into the house. "Santa's funny," says Kaley.

"He sure is," I say. I look at the mailbox. 2013. This'll be one to come back to. I drive on a little, slow down in front of a display that has just a couple of trees lit up with strings of multi-colored lights. These can often be old people who have a lot of stuff, poor security and not much strength to put up resistance if they do wake up. Not that we'd ever seriously hurt someone. "Do you like the trees?" I ask Kaley.

She says, "Yeah," in a quiet, reserved way. I try to make eye contact with Liz, but she's looking out the windows. "How about you, Mommy?"

She hums for just a few seconds, then says, "I think they look nice." I look at the address. 2027. There was one house in between the two that we might check out, but, more likely, we'll just do those two. It's not a good idea to do too many in a row. I notice that I think "we", but, tonight, it'll just be me so that Liz can sleep with the kids. She's better at catching the little things that we could pick up, but I'm a little quicker in terms of getting in and getting out.

I drive a bit, then roll to a stop in front of a house with those wire animatronic reindeer that look like they're eating. Kaley says, "It looks like Rudolph." I quickly write down the two addresses and we move along. For the first time this season, I wonder if Jimmy has some kind of suspicion that Liz and I come back to these houses. It doesn't seem likely to me, but it's hard to tell. I wonder if him not getting it makes him gullible. Everything about my son is getting less and less readable to me.

There's a strange set of lights on the other side of the road. It looks like it's supposed to be a UFO. Or maybe a tank where the cannon won't stay on. Either way, it doesn't seem very Christmasy. This might be a house we'd break into on principle. "What do you think that is?" I ask.

I peek into the rearview mirror, and I see that Jimmy actually does look up, though only quickly. He doesn't give an answer, and he must not be curious enough to look up again. After a few seconds of quiet, Liz says, "Maybe it's a big Christmas bulb".

Jimmy says, "Looks like a hamburger." It's possible that he's right, though that's not really any more like Christmas than a UFO or a cannonless tank. "Could be," Liz says. "Think it has pickles?" I ask.

Kaley twists in her seat, trying to look for green, but I can't tell if she can actually see what's behind her or not. "Dylan Mueller puts barbecue sauce on his hamburgers when we have them for lunch," Jimmy says. This is a rare moment of sharing, even if it's about something so mundane. I check and Liz is running her fingers through Kaley's hair. "To each their own," she says. Kaley starts to tilt her head towards Liz's shoulder. She's tired, which is fine. Over the course of tonight, we already have six or seven possible houses to go back and visit, so we should be in good shape. Kaley will pick out clothes for school tomorrow, part of her goodnight ritual. There's a good chance it'll be one of the dresses we've stolen for her. Liz had the idea to check in people's laundry rooms for clothes.

The laundry rooms are almost always by the outside of the home, easy to get into. If you see a home that you can tell has kids, you can pop in quickly before a larger house, take a couple of decent looking outfits and get out. But you have to be careful not to do something that would draw attention before hitting another home, and you can't take something that looks custom made, or your kid will be a target at school, and you'll get busted. If you're smart and careful, you can do it. We haven't bought new clothes for the kids in a little over a year. We always tell them that we go shopping while they're in school.

I look back again, "Jimmy, did you finish your report on Benjamin Franklin?" He doesn't answer, which is his answer. This complicates things not so much because we'll be scrambling to help him. That's not a big deal. It's more that it upsets the balance of how tonight will run. It was supposed to be: get home, have some Christmas cookies, put Kaley to bed, finish homework with Jimmy, put him to bed, then Liz wraps gifts while I go out and get some more. A simple, predictable plan. Sadly, these sorts of hiccups are becoming more and more common for Jimmy. Thanksgiving weekend, Liz was supposed to do a little purse picking during Black Friday, but Jimmy said that he had to take care of a display of Indians that he was supposed to have finished the day before Thanksgiving break. Liz ended up sitting over his shoulder and coaching him while he downloaded some graphics. I took Kaley to the park for a while. Technically, I could've kept Kaley and helped Jimmy, but we feel it's important to show Jimmy that he needs to do his work, and we don't like to punish Kaley for Jimmy's mistakes.

"Who's Benjamin Frankman?" Kaley asks. Liz kisses the top of her head. "By tomorrow, Jimmy will be able to tell you all about Benjamin Franklin."

Kaley says, "Oh forget it," and Liz and I try not to laugh too hard. "How about one more block, and then we'll head home." Jimmy doesn't say anything. Kaley leans back into Liz, and that's about it. I could've said that we'd go straight home, but it would've been like giving in to Jimmy. We see a couple of pretty flat, white lights on the eaves of roofs. Having Jimmy is a little like having a preview for where Kaley might be heading. I think she'll be easier in a lot of ways, but I still feel a little dread thinking about it. I know it's cliché, but she's my princess.

"Eeesh," I say. "Santa looks a little down." Everybody looks out the window to see a half-inflated balloon Santa. He's deflated enough to look like he's bent over. "Why is Santa like that?" Kaley asks. Before Liz or I can answer, Jimmy says, "He's waiting for his boyfriend." Liz and I are quiet, but Kaley giggles. "Santa doesn't have a boyfriend," she says. I'm pretty sure that Jimmy doesn't actually know what he's referring to, but I can't be sure. There is the possibility that someone has explained it to him, but it seems hard to believe that he'd really get it yet. The actual mechanics of sex. I remember sex seeming very abstract at his age. I knew that something went on, but wasn't totally sure what it was that grown up men and women did. Probably I would've been grossed out.

"Jimmy is being not nice," says Liz, "probably because he's ashamed that he didn't finish his homework." Liz has a knack for oversimplifying our psyches in a way that can be deflating. Luckily for us, she only uses this power for good, like cutting off any further explanation from Jimmy. "The Santa balloon is falling over because the cold from outside is making the air inside him get smaller," I say. "It's something that you'll learn about in science class in a couple of years." I feel stupid, having said it. "Everyone gets a little down when it's cold," I say. There's total quiet from the back. I wish that Liz would say something that could pick me back up. Maybe she thinks that I should've been on top of Ben Franklin before this late in the evening. She'd be right. It makes me wonder, again, if Jimmy knows what we do. If he were doing this to keep us from stealing, there would be something sweet about that, but that seems impossible to me. His rebellion would almost have to be stealing himself. What will we say when that starts?

"What cookies are you guys having?" I ask. Kaley puts her hands up and says, "Frosted." Jimmy sighs. "Do I get cookies, or am I punished for the report?" Liz looks out the window. "Maybe you can have one while you finish your report, which you'll do on your own this time." I'm a little surprised by this, but it's probably the right thing to do. She's usually right when it comes to things like this.

"Another Rudolph," Liz says, which both smooths things out and ends the conversation. I put in a Christmas CD that I got from this little Cape Cod home that had these blinking light-up icicles hanging from the eaves. It was weird, sorting through their CDs, being in their living room next to a turned-off Christmas tree. Trying to take just enough stuff to have them not call the authorities or push hard to pursue things. We're lucky we haven't had so much as a brush with the law yet.

The first song is "Santa Claus is Coming to Town." I feel like I should skip to the next track instead of making everyone listen to us being told that we should watch out and not pout, but I let it go. I take couple of turns that'll get us home faster but miss some displays. Even over the CD, I can hear Kaley's breathing starting to slow. I like getting to carry her into the house when she's sleepy. There's something reassuring about the weight of a little person that depends on you. It's the weight of your love and obligation. When I'm breaking into a house, a lot of times I operate under this stupid assumption that God won't let either Liz or me get caught because we're watching over these two children, even though we're the ones who wanted kids. When Kaley fatigues and I carry her off, I feel protected, when Jimmy blows off his report, I feel like things might crash. And for good reason. As we near our home, I feel rest-less, which isn't necessarily a good mindset, if I'm going to go back out tonight. "What was your favorite display?" I ask. "Hamburger," says Kaley, giggling. "I liked the moving reindeer," says Liz, which is what she always says. Jimmy is quiet for a bit. I have no interest in pressing him, but Liz says, "Jimmy?" Out my window, I see what I know is a doctor's house, and I wish that I could get in and take his cufflinks or golf clubs or whatever might be worth a lot, but I'm always nervous that those are the homes that are going to have serious security systems or other unpredictable barriers. You always have to watch out for signs of a dog.

"Bent over Santa," Jimmy says. I turn my head just a bit, and although he doesn't say anything, I can tell he knows. I look back at the road and make the final turn, just five blocks from home. "What was yours, Papa?" Liz asks. I think about it for a couple of seconds. I end up pulling into the driveway before I answer. I turn off the car and say, "I think I liked the Christmas donkey."

Kaley laughs. "Christmas Donkey?" I turn back and pretend to pinch her nose. She puts her hands over her face and buries it in Liz's side. I make eye contact with Jimmy, and he puts his Gameboy in his pocket. I'm trying to remember where we stole it from, and it occurs to me that we might have actually bought that one. I want to tell him how much it costs, but I have no clue, and I know it wouldn't matter. Even though she's awake now, I get out and go to pick up Kaley. Once again, I'm glad for her. I'd pay anything to get her something. Or, I'd do what it takes to get it for her, which really isn't the same thing. As I carry her into our own house, I'm glad to see that our things are safe, that our kids can sleep soundly in a warm house. I look at Liz, who smiles at me, even if I'm not sure quite what that means.

"You're A Mother"

Stephenson looks at one of the mothers from his daughter's school and tries not to shake his head. The mother, is wearing leather pants and one of those shirts that shows her midriff. The problem with this is that she has worn this to an elementary school's open house night. Stephenson thinks about the saying about being a Republican when you get older. He doesn't remember exactly how it goes, and he doesn't totally agree with it, but he does realize that his reaction is more conservative than it would have been a few years ago. Even now, maybe, if Stephenson didn't have a grade-school-age daughter, he might look at this woman and be glad that she was willing to walk around in public with a bit of her tummy showing and her shirt tight enough to put her breasts on display. But, now, he looks at her and thinks about her son's school experience. "You're a mother," he wants to say.

He knows her son, a little. Stephenson had talked to her son some on the school field trip last year. He's not a bad kid. One of those boys with a mohawk and t-shirts that Stephenson wouldn't buy if it was his son. But he was kind of quiet, and he didn't argue with the adults or the other kids. Stephenson feels like that validates his suspicions about the mother's inappropriate clothing. The son doesn't assert himself like the other kids do. What will the son say to his mother as he gets older?

Stephenson runs his hand along his daughter's hair. She's wearing a t-shirt with two cupcakes and a heart on it. "I like your wolf," he tells her, pointing to a drawing hanging on the wall. Wolves are the mascot of his daughter's school. His daughter has put a pink bow above her wolf's ear. His daughter looks bored, but there are supposed to be cookies soon.

Stephenson's wife is talking to the teacher about how much homework is appropriate for their daughter to be bringing home. This was the plan going into tonight. Some nights, his daughter has three sheets of homework, some nights she has none. This does not match what their daughter's best friend brings home, which is exactly one sheet of homework per night. All of this is like the world's worst math problem to Stephenson. His wife seems to think that there is some sort of conspiracy against their daughter. Stephenson suspects that the teacher is simply incompetent. But he can't articulate this suspicion to his wife in a way that doesn't bring on more problems. At work, Stephenson is articulate. He is in charge of monitoring safety, and he can explain OSHA standards, issues with insurance and related matters. Even playing with his daughter, he can usually get a giggle. But Stephenson has trouble being clear when he has to triangulate among himself, other adults and his daughter. For now, Stephenson kneels down and whispers into his daughter's ear, "Where does your school keep the monkeys?"

His daughter smiles, but doesn't start laughing yet. "No monkeys," she says.

Stephenson keeps a straight face. "Your principal said that they'd taught the monkeys to roller skate for the parents."

Stephenson's daughter tugs on his arm. "Daddeee…" she says, "monkeys can't roller skate."

Stephenson shakes his head. "I'm pretty sure," he says. "Your principal said that they could roller skate and that they'd have sparkle wands so that it would be bright and shiny all over the halls."

Now his daughter laughs a little. She's still bored, but she's kind of tired and feeling silly. "School doesn't have monkeys."

Stephenson is quiet for a few seconds. His wife is listening to the teacher talk. "Maybe your principal said pigs instead of monkeys."

His daughter laughs harder now. "Daddy, pigs can't roller skate either."

Stephenson rubs his daughter's belly. "Maybe it was flying carpets instead of roller skates."

***

There are other mothers that Stephenson notices. For instance, the pale little boy who always brings organic food in his lunch has a thin mother who Stephenson might find attractive if she wasn't so serious. Not that he would ever make a move. Stephenson is married. But it makes him think about what kind of woman his daughter will be. Stephenson wants her to be strong, but there are different ways that women can be strong, and he doesn't think that he would want his daughter to be strong in the way that this mother is strong. It's hard, for instance, to imagine having sex with her. He doesn't want to be like a fratboy and assume that all women who are strong or are feminists are automatically frigid, but he also feels like she is more focused on "good" than she is on how to have fun or allow anyone else to have fun.

But maybe her seriousness works as a kind of shield, keeping the horniest and dumbest men away in order to keep from being sexually assaulted or harassed. But there's a sadness, there, too. Stephenson has met this woman's husband. He's not a bad guy, but he is not anyone to be excited by. He talks about NPR and politics a lot. He fits the wife well, Stephenson supposes, but it's hard for him to imagine the two of them having had a romantic courtship. It's almost like their lukewarm courtship is what resulted in the pale child, though that's pure conjecture on Stephenson's part.

Still, if Stephenson had to pick a role model for his daughter, he would pick the serious woman over the mother who shows her midriff. It wouldn't even be close. Not that Stephenson's wife is a bad role model, but "role model" doesn't seem an accurate descriptor for a parent. Too often, children think of what they'll do differently than their parents rather than what they'll imitate. Stephenson does not have a particular distrust of or complaint about his parents, but he still notices what he does and doesn't do like his own father. He watches less football and buys more "collectibles" than his father did. And maybe that's not so different from the midriff-bearing mom. He doesn't seem his age, or not like his father did, anyway. But it still seems like buying a few action figures is not the same as dressing like a tramp.

***

Today, Stephenson had the day off, and he is picking up his daughter from school. The midriff mother and the serious mother are both waiting outside the school with him. Not with him, of course, but in the same general area. The midriff mother is wearing a tank-top and jean short cutoffs. Stephenson tries not to look very much. When he was single, he would have checked her out without being self conscious. But when she is the mother of a child who will be walking out the same door that his own daughter walks out, things are just different. Plus, the serious mother is there, and Stephenson is fairly certain that she would say something to him, or at least glare at him, if she noticed that Stephenson was looking at the midriff mom, even though the midriff mom is dressing in such a provocative way.

And this is the core of what unsettles Stephenson. This woman, whose ass cheeks hang out from the bottom of her shorts, is talking on a cell phone, seemingly oblivious to any men checking her out, but also oblivious to the fact that her dress has an impact upon all women, particularly young women. Stephenson wants to walk up to her and tell her that her bad choices are making things harder for his daughter. And yet, would he only make things harder for this woman's son? Not because the mother would go home and abuse her son, but because it would cause a scene, and it might carry tension for the rest of the school year, if not for the rest of his daughter's stay at the school. So Stephenson is stuck in a very strange space. In order to protect his daughter, he has to not stand up for women, but his standing up for women would actually be confronting a woman, and part of his reaction to this woman is determined by another woman that he does not see as a good model for women. The logic is dizzying.

Stephenson pulls out his own cell phone. He brings up his

primary e-mail. There are a few e-mails from his co-workers addressing concerns that people are raising about a possible OSHA visit. There are also a few forwards that have come from Stephenson's mother. Jokes ridiculing contemporary political figures, no doubt. While Stephenson is checking his e-mail, he hears the midriff mother saying, "He can choke on a dick, for all I care."

Stephenson tries very hard not to show that he looks at the serious mother. She might be frowning, but it always seems like she might be frowning. Stephenson scrolls up and down his e-mail, not opening any more messages. The midriff mother starts laughing. Then, she says, "Fucking A."

Stephenson makes sure that he does not move his eyes from his phone. The midriff mother says another curse word. He listens for the serious mother, but she says nothing. Stephenson feels deeply disappointed. When he looks up, he does not see either of the mothers, he sees the back doors of the school opening. The first kids out of the door are the kindergarteners. They are loud and they stumble out of the doors, sometimes bumping into each other and sometimes running off a bit. The aides tell the students to watch where they're going, and they point them to their parents' cars.

The midriff mother is laughing now. It sounds like a bad laugh. Like the kind of laugh that a theater student would do in an introductory level course where the student is supposed to play a horrible villain in a children's play. Now, Stephenson does look at the serious mother. She is looking directly at the other mother. Stephenson wishes that she would say something. He wishes that she would read the midriff mother the riot act. But he realizes, now, looking at her, that she won't.

When Stephenson's daughter comes out of the school, he walks towards her quickly, then he picks her up. His hands slide in between her back and her backpack, and he squeezes her tightly. "How was your day?" he asks. Stephenson brings his daughter to his car, walking past both mothers. His daughter tells him about PE, where they learned how to play a new kind of tag. Stephenson knows that one of the PE teacher's tricks is to basically teach tag or freeze tag with different names and references. During winter, she teaches them "ice giants and princesses tag". During spring, she teaches them "flowers and raindrops tag". Around Valentine's Day, she teaches them "Cupid tag". But Stephenson is not about to spoil his daughter's day. She seems happy to talk about this new kind of tag. This is "Leprechaun Tag", because St. Patrick's Day was not long ago.

There is some chatter behind Stephenson as he brings his daughter back to the car. Stephenson will probably never be sure, but he hopes that the serious mother is telling the midriff mother that what she's saying is inappropriate. It's possible that Stephenson would hear from another parent that there was a big dust-up after school and that, even if he didn't hear the specific names, he would know who was involved. Stephenson realizes, buckling his daughter into her car seat, that he doesn't know the midriff mother's name, though he's pretty sure that he knows the serious mother's last name, but not her first name. Still, as he gets into his seat and puts his key in the ignition, as he starts his car and checks his rearview mirror, Stephenson starts to realize that maybe he's setting his daughter up for the happy medium. Not the tightass with the pale son and not the ass-showing mother who might embarrass her son.

But he still doesn't quite feel good. He knows that's not quite fair; it's just that he hasn't quite figured out what is.

Bigfoot

Alex was sitting in a folding chair and whistling, which Drew took as a sign of primitive aggression. The whistling was always murder on Drew's headaches. It might've been better than listening to him talk about the need for a vegetarian UFC champ, but not that much. Drew couldn't tell what song or group it was. It might've been punk, given the fast pace and repetitive rhythm. At least Alex was stuffed up enough today to need a pause now and then. There was still a big chunk of fliers to get on the clipboards for the ALO demonstration. That was because they'd knocked off early last night to go catch a show. Some local band Emily had heard of. Drew couldn't remember who exactly, but it was one of those bands with a swear word in their name, and the swear word was a gerund. Emily loved those kinds of bands. That and the kind of bands that wore masks and had clips of factory sounds playing in the background.

Drew had wanted to go out and do something about the Bigfoot situation, but Emily said they couldn't really do anything that night anyway, and she wasn't going to stick around getting bogus information from the mainstream media all night. She was right. Even the blogs were all over the place with weird information and claims.

There were dozens of reports that Bigfoot was already dead, over ten that Bigfoot was an alien, and even a few weirder ones, like that someone was making an anti-cancer drug from Bigfoot's droppings or that he would only eat live chickens. Alex said that report was actually cut and pasted from an old article about Ozzy Osbourne. Still, the whole night, all Drew could think about was that sad look from Bigfoot. It was the only footage that'd been released to the public, and it was everywhere. Lady Gaga had already announced that she'd be working it into her next video and tour.

"I think," said Drew, "that we should just ask for immediate release. If he's kept in captivity, then just like any other animal, any other being—"

"Drew," said Emily, crossing her legs, "did you hear for sure what the gender of the Bigfoot is yet?"

Drew's mouth twitched. Emily could turn at the drop of a hat. He looked down at the petition sheets. "Sorry. I meant 'he or she.'"

Emily was working on the signs; her art was getting better all the time. Alex leaned back on the feet of his chair. "Immediate release, huh?" Maybe he'd been thinking about the layout for tomorrow's demonstration or about animal release in general, but Drew doubted it.

"Well, it's just that if we're already against zoos. Where they have him has to be way worse than a zoo. Maybe worse than a cosmetics-testing lab. Right?" Drew knuckled his temple. "Probably worse, I bet."

Emily drew a few squiggles in the air. She'd been trying to incorporate more primitive art into her protests lately. Drew couldn't remember if she'd said that was trying to be more in tune with the planet or if she was gunning for an NEA grant. Maybe both. "Yeah. But if we focus on springing just Bigfoot rather than zoo animals in general, then people will say that we're anthropocentric, that we're focusing our efforts on the most human animal we can find, because, deep down, we think humans are the highest form of animal just like most people do."

Alex let his front legs drop onto the floor. He did this Charlie Chaplin thing where he pretended to look as surprised as anyone. Or maybe it was a Buster Keaton thing. .

"Maybe," Drew said, "but we could pull people in with Bigfoot who might not support other animal causes. Besides, a lot of the older wolves from the ALO helped out on stuff like the Mumia campaign or free Tibet, and that didn't compromise our animal-rights principles."

"Yeah, and Bigfoot didn't even murder anybody," said Alex.

Emily's giggles turned to a frown. "Mumia didn't kill anyone, except maybe in self-defense. And, Drew, the point isn't whether or not our principles are compromised. We have to be mindful of how our actions make people think of our activism and our cause." Emily was wearing a shirt with a graphic that she'd scratched a little and reworked to say Fugazi, but Drew couldn't tell what it had originally said.

Alex stood up and pulled out a handkerchief. It was one of those blue, mass-produced hankies that made Drew think of redneck factory workers. "You know," Alex said. "Even if they do release Bigfoot, Bigfoot'll never actually be free." Alex laughed and shook his head. "There'll be 24-hour-a-day coverage for as long as someone can get ratings or some kind of merchandising income."

"And there could be poachers," said Emily.

"Poachers?" Alex blew his nose while he went to the window. "Bigfoot will be monitored way too closely to get knocked off by some nutjob looking to get on the cover of Guns & Ammo."

Emily took the cap off a new marker. They'd tried to buy some eco-friendly art supplies, but the posters would smear on the way to the rallies, so they'd gone back to the mass produced stuff, even though they all felt like jerks buying it. "Alive or dead, someone would probably say it'd make great television. FOX, I bet."

That got a little chuckle from all three. "Nike would sponsor it," said Emily. She drew a swoosh in the air. "Big shoes for big feet."

Alex unfolded his hankie and looked at it. "Well, if they give Bigfoot a show and the ratings fell, then maybe they would let the Nuge have a crack at him."

As they finished laughing, Drew started loading clipboards into the box to bring to the protest. "Really, though. Bigfoot. Isn't it crazy?"

"I thought it was a hoax," said Emily.

Alex sat down and wiped his upper lip. "I thought I'd tuned in to an Onion radio broadcast at first. No shit. I almost pissed my pants when I figured out it was true." Alex put the handkerchief on his leg. It was kind of crumpled. Hankies were a little more environmentally friendly than tissues, but Drew still thought they were gross. The planet was the most important thing, but it seemed to him that there should've been some happy medium between eco-friendliness and taking care of Alex's seasonal allergies. Drew said, "I heard this group in the Midwest is trying to appropriate 'beast' like the gay people did for 'queer'. They're trying to make porn based on rutting movements."

"Porn is bad, period," said Emily. "And beasts bite your head off for no good reason."

Alex snorted. "So do liberal chicks if you don't listen to their poetry."

Emily slid the marker in her hand so that she was holding it like a knife. "Fuck you; I may be an artist, but I don't write crappy poetry. And 'beast' creates a certain idea in people's minds that animals, especially neglected animals, don't need."

Drew wiped his forehead with his wrist; every time he got hungover, he would sweat like only a human could. "Do you want some of that wine we picked up during the alpaca protest?"

This led them to both look over at Alex. He held up his hands and shrugged. "I told you guys before, you don't have to check with me every time. Just chill out and I'll be fine."

"We know," said Emily. "We just want to be sensitive."

"You rub my face in it a lot more by asking me than if you'd just get plowed like you're supposed to." After a few seconds of quiet, Alex finished, "Hey, we're supposed to be advocating rights, not suppressing them, right?" He grinned.

Emily got up from the table. "I'll go get us some wine. Alex, want coffee?"

He looked toward the window in the front of the headquarters. Drew waited for him to pitch some new sign for their headquarters, something involving violence, lesbians or both. "Sure," was all that he said.

As Emily went into the back room for coffee and wine, Drew went over to the supply cupboard and grabbed three mugs. One of them had a dead bug in it. Drew frowned and blew the little body out of it. It knocked against the side of the cup and flew out onto the floor. He wiped the inside of the cup with his finger. When he turned back, Alex was looking at him. Drew smiled and gave him a mug that hadn't had anything in it. "You know," said Alex, "Emily isn't as interested in me as you think she is."

Drew took his and Emily's mug back to the table where she'd been working. He kept the bug mug for himself. "Oh."

"Just thought you might want to know that."

Drew put a large rubber band around several of the full clipboards, making sure that each clipboard alternated top and bottom to conserve space. Alex leaned back in his chair again, but this time he let it down slowly. Drew could feel his face getting hot. Sweat was starting to drip. "You really think that you and Em hooking up is going to make a difference in the cause as a whole?"

Drew let the end of his clipboard clank down on the table. His head was throbbing. "Alex," he said. "The fact that we act is predicated on the idea that each individual can make a difference to the whole. It might be a small difference, but it matters, and if things didn't work out, then it's entirely possible that we might not be able to work together. What if ALO loses a great artist like her?"

Alex shook his head. "Sometimes you think too much, man. A little fucking might renew your enthusiasm for the cause."

Drew dropped the clipboard. Before he could do anything other than pick it up, Emily walked back in with an open bottle of wine. "Coffee'll be up in a minute, Alex."

"No hurry," said Alex. He looked back towards the window. Drew held up his mug for Emily to pour in the wine. He waited for the mug to get more than half full before saying "when." As Emily picked up her mug and went back to her posters, Drew held the mug up to his nose. The wine smelled tart. He looked at the mug. It had a picture of Mickey Mouse on it, and Drew wondered where they'd gotten it from. "It's good," he said, before trying any of the wine. When he did take a sip, that little hair of the dog made him feel pleasantly warm instead of just hot. He wondered if Bigfoot ingested any kind of intoxicant. It wasn't a purely human practice.

Emily took a sip of her wine. "It's all right." She held her mug in the air, away from her, as she kept doodling on the poster. She tilted her head. Her neck looked long and elegant. Like something that you'd touch lightly to feel it without leaving a mark. "Maybe," said Drew, "we should focus on getting them to feed Bigfoot a vegetarian diet. I mean, if Bigfoot's system can handle it, and if Bigfoot's close to human in biology then it should be okay, and when the being flourishes with a vegetarian diet it could be big." "I'm telling you," said Alex, "You get one UFC fighter to be veg while holding a belt, and every fratboy in America will leave meat behind."

"Yeah," said Emily, "that's our demographic."

Alex shook his head. "Whey protein ain't murder like meat, yo."

Emily looked up from her sign. "Maybe Bigfoot already is an herbivore. It's not so uncommon for primates. Have either of you heard any announcements about dietary findings?"

Drew frowned. He wondered if Emily and Alex had ever fucked. Alex said, "You'd sure think somebody would be on that. They have to be monitoring what the big thing's eating fairly carefully. Can you imagine the explosion that would happen if they captured Bigfoot and ended up killing the poor fucker?"

Drew shook his head. It chilled him to even think of that as possible. Emily set her mug down quickly and a bit loudly. Drew worried that she'd stain her poster. "Although, think of how much it would strengthen our argument against zoos and captivity in general if Bigfoot did die in captivity."

"You want Bigfoot to die?" asked Alex.

Emily looked down at her poster. "Of course not. I wish every living being well. But, maybe if Bigfoot just got sick or something. Then when they released Bigfoot back into the wild..."

After a brief silence, Alex stood up. "I'll go check the coffee."

After he left, Emily looked over to Drew. "You understand what I'm saying, don't you?"

"Just a second," Drew said. He was counting his stack of petitions for the third time. It would be a tragedy if a great creature died only to end up as backdrop to Lady Gaga for a national tour. Drew had always imagined Bigfoot as being big and majestic, but this thing had been bent, and its fur might've had shit in it. In a way, if it didn't have shit, that should be a red flag. "Umm..." he said, still staring at the stack.

"I'm not saying I want him dead," said Emily. "Or her." She ran a hand through her hair, getting a touch of marker on her cheek. "I'm not going to try to assassinate Bigfoot or something. That would just make me a hunter."

Drew looked from the stack over to her. "Emily, I know you'd never kill Bigfoot."

"Hunh," said Emily. She went back to her poster and Alex came in with his coffee and with a cigarette between his lips. He blew on his coffee and swirled his mug very slowly. "I bet people start looking twice as hard for the Loch Ness Monster because of the Bigfoot capture. Has anyone heard any announcements about that?"

Emily shook her head. "I bet you're right. " She held up the poster she'd been working on. The sign read: "Meat is murder / Zoos are torture", and it had a picture of a teddy bear crying behind bars. All the letters were empty frames of red with dotted insides. The tagboard started to fold over a little as Emily held it up. "Ach," she said, and she set down her wine. "When someone's holding it two handed at the protest it'll stay up. You know the ban on posts and sticks to keep signs up has totally fucked with the way we do our posters?"

Drew nodded. "Looks good to me, Em. Have you thought about just leaving the little letters spotted? Gives a nice texture to it."

Alex snickered. Drew looked at him. "What?"

"Yeah," said Emily. "It's not that bad." She tossed a marker at Alex, and the tag board sagged again. The marker bounced off his chest and landed in his coffee. Emily stomped her feet and cheered.

"Shit," Alex said. Drew snickered. After getting another stack of clipboards banded and in the box, Drew said, "I like the sign."

"Thank you, Drew," said Emily. She let the poster drift down to the table again. It made him think of a commercial, something for soap or an expensive pair of designer jeans. "It might be a little too cutesy, but I think people are getting tired of the really graphic posters. I don't want to get compared to those pro-lifers."

"Fuckers," said Alex. He fished the marker out of his coffee, sniffed the contents of his mug, and took a sip.

Drew shook his hands out, trying to loosen them up after all the stacking and counting. "It might pay to be mindful of that stuff.

We don't want to undercut everything we do with some bad associations. Or even just making the same mistakes that other activists might make."

Alex sighed. "We define ourselves with each action and activism. Because of my AA shit, I can define myself each moment." He took a drag off his cigarette. "I'm an alcoholic, but each day my actions prove me to be sober."

Drew bent some of his fingers back a little, just to stretch. "Is your sponsor an activist, Alex?"

Alex smiled and narrowed his eyes. "Are you fucking with me?"

There was a knock on the door. The three of them looked at each other and then Alex stood up. "Don't worry, I'm sure it's not the Feds."

Emily said, "Maybe it's your sponsor, coming to join up and fight the good fight with us."

Alex nodded. "Or maybe it's your parents coming to see what all the money they put into art school has done."

Drew shook his head and his hands, giving a little grunt of disapproval. They all glared at each other, and then the knock came again. "I'm coming," yelled Alex as he went to the door.

Before the door was even fully open, Grenadine came bursting in. Her legs got bound up in the skirt she wore over her jeans, and she stumbled a little. As she righted herself, she yelled, "Bigfoot's pregnant!"

Drew tried to think about his breathing. The appropriate response to this was important, and he felt a bit hungover to know if he should yell or nod solemnly. Either seemed reasonable. This put a whole new level of concern for the care Bigfoot (now obviously a she) received while in captivity. Drew looked up to see Emily and Grenadine jumping up and down.

Alex shook his head and laughed. "Somebody get to work on knitting some bigass booties."

"I can't believe there's gonna be more Bigfoots," said Emily. She hugged Grenadine. "Let's have some wine to celebrate."

Drew scooted his chair back. "There'll only be more if the babies are carried to term. Babies, hell, does anyone even know how many children a Bigfoot mother has? Or the gestation period?" Drew put a hand over his eyes. He felt hot, and his head hurt.

Emily quit jumping and started laughing. "Jesus, Drew, you can't even be happy about more Bigfoots?" She did a twirl. "You should quit worrying about some of that shit and clap and laugh and drink or smoke up more."

"I'm drinking," said Drew.

"That's a good first step," Alex said. "But you haven't even tried 'shrooms before."

Grenadine grabbed the bottle of wine. "Yeah, be happy, Drew. A preggers Bigfoot. Who would've thought we'd live to see that?"

All Drew could think of was a whole other generation of Bigfoots to look sad for the camera. How long would it be before they made a string of awful movies about it and forced the Bigfoot family to go on the Today Show to promote them? "I guess. It's just, there are just so many new questions and worries, I guess."

"Yeah," said Alex, "like what if Bigfoot wants an abortion?" They all looked at Alex. "What if Bigfoot's a lesbian, was raped by some other Bigfoot, and doesn't want to carry it to term?" He smirked as the rest of them stared. "Just joking." After a pause and some drinking from the others, Alex said, "Hey, I got a real question for you, Drew: suppose a hunter came along, ready to murder Bigfoot. Murder a pregnant Bigfoot. Do you think you could take the hunter out to save the Bigfoot?"

"Oh Christ," said Grenadine. She walked over to Alex and grabbed his cigarette. "All your jokes and hypotheticals. Who cares? Bigfoot's pregnant. And that means there's a male Bigfoot. A probable male Bigfoot and a definite pregnant fucking female." She took a very long drag.

Alex shook his head and puffed out his lip. "No, no. Bigfoot was fucking. Now she's pregnant."

Emily flipped him off. Alex shrugged and pulled out another cigarette. "Whatever. Just asking about the hunters."

Drew nodded. "Yeah, it's a good question. That and whether or not they'll go after that male Bigfoot."

Alex shrugged. "If they don't, then it's the breakdown of the Bigfoot family unit."

"Knock it off. And it's not a good question." Emily went back to her posters. "Drew, why would you be the one person between Bigfoot and a hunter? And why would you have a gun?"

"But it doesn't matter," he put his clipboard and sheets down to finish his wine. "The point of the question isn't to get the answer; it's to force me to consider where I fit into the movement. Plus, you never know. I'm sure none of us ever thought there'd be a Bigfoot capture and confinement, but here we are."

Grenadine laughed. "Yeah, Em. What if Bigfoot got cancer, and they gave her chemo and radiation? Would you share some pot with her to help her get her appetite back?"

Emily tightened her face. "Only after she gave birth."

Alex laughed. After a little silence, Drew asked, "Really, guys, what do you think we should do?"

"Do?" asked Alex. "We really can't do anything right now. Busting her out is impossible, and wouldn't actually do anything anyway. Are we going to demand she be released so that she can get captured again? Or dogged by scientists and documentarians?"

Emily underlined the words "murder" and "Torture". "Bullshit. We are doing something." She held up her poster. "I'm doing something, and Drew is doing something. What are you doing, Alex?"

Alex looked out the window. "Nothing. I'm doing nothing. Just another member of the animal kingdom living in captivity."

Drew shivered. He thought of Bigfoot having to nurse her offspring in front of all those scientists. "All Bigfoot's kids are going to be born into captivity. Every last one of them."

Grenadine drank straight from the bottle of wine. "We should check the website and our e-mail. See what ALO's official stance is. Figure out if we can tie that in to tomorrow's demonstration somehow."

"Sure," said Drew. "Who would our ALO contact be?"

They all looked around. There was an awkward silence as they all realized that they had no access to ALO's inside information. Emily was the first to give up, filling in her letters, then Grenadine tested out the bullhorns, singing old protest songs and finally Drew went back to his clipboards. He tried to think of something to whistle, but he kept coming up with old TV show themes, and that didn't seem appropriate.

As the rest of them went about their work, Alex smoked his

cigarette. "We ought to start a garden to work in. Bring some life into this place, you know?"

"That sounds fine," said Emily. "We could always use the extra life."

Nobody else responded. Alex turned the radio to a folk-hip-hop fusion song. Nobody acknowledged his choice.

All the Different Dangers of Cars

Taylor turns the key in the ignition. Her boyfriend's car is a little louder than her mother's. Her stepfather and her mother's car, really, but she would only ever call it her mother's car. Her boyfriend sits in the passenger's seat. Taylor is in the driver's seat because her boyfriend, Bobby, is too drunk to drive. He's singing something, but he's mumbling the lyrics, so she can't tell what exactly. Taylor thinks that she will drive Bobby to his home, but she's not entirely sure what she'll do when she gets there. If she brings Bobby to his front door as drunk as he is, then he'll get in trouble, and he'll tell her that she shouldn't have done it. But she can't bring him to her house either. Taylor looks in the rearview mirror. A few cars go back and forth past the driveway, but not that many. Taylor reaches her right hand behind the passenger's seat and looks back. The driveway must be at least four times as long as Bobby's car, but she's only had one beer, and she knows that she can manage it.

Taylor puts the car in reverse and backs down the driveway. Her stepfather would be proud. At least, Taylor thinks he would. Her stepfather is who taught her how to drive. Taylor's mother only drives if she absolutely has to. Once, when Taylor was throwing up, and Taylor's stepfather was at work, Taylor's mother took her to urgent care, but that was only because it was an emergency. Taylor hopes that Bobby doesn't throw up in the car. "I'll fucking have it," Bobby says. Taylor is not sure what Bobby thinks he'll be getting. She takes a deep breath and tries to keep the car straight as she backs down the driveway. Taylor veers a little to the left, then overcompensates, but then she does get herself down the middle. She's almost perfectly centered when a car going by honks its horn. Taylor stomps on the break. Bobby falls forward. He mumbles some more curse words, then just slumps forward. "Shit," Taylor says.

***

When Taylor was learning how to drive, it was hard to focus, because she wasn't used to her stepfather. Her stepfather yelled less than her father, but at least her father was predictable. He lost his temper easily, and it wasn't always for a good reason, but you could always watch him and know exactly what he thought. Taylor's stepfather was different. He was like a robot that got quietly annoyed instead of angry.

As they drove, Taylor would get nervous, watching other drivers but also trying to watch her stepfather to see if he was shaking his head, watching the speedometer or just glaring at Taylor. In the end, he actually didn't even seem to be paying attention some of the time. Sometimes, he'd say something like "Doing fine," but mostly he'd just stare ahead at the road while Taylor tried to figure out what to do. Sometimes, her stepfather would point and say, "Turn here," but that was just to practice turning, it wasn't to get her anywhere in particular.

128

Bobby is trying to roll his window down. "What the fuck are you doing?" Taylor asks.

"Gotta puke," Bobby tells her. Taylor can't watch, because cars are going by, but she also knows that Bobby will be angry if he wakes up tomorrow and there's puke all over his car. Even if it's his puke.

"Just let me pull over," Taylor says.

Bobby waves his hands all over. "No," he says, "they'll think that you've been drinking, too. Don't do it."

Taylor sighs. Bobby is usually a good boyfriend. At least, he's funny, he hasn't cheated on her, and he knows where the good parties are. Then again, tonight was a good party, and here Taylor is, driving home. "Just hold it," Taylor says, but Bobby leans hard out of his window, and he pukes along the road. Taylor thinks about slamming on the breaks so that Bobby will slam his head on the side mirror, but she decides that the best thing to do is to drop Bobby off and get home before she's in too much trouble. Taylor checks the time on the clock. By the time she gets home, Taylor will probably miss her curfew. Tonight is one of the many times that Taylor wishes she had her own house. No stepfather. No next-morning questions. With her own place, Taylor would be able to take Bobby home, put him to bed, and have a good night's sleep. She'd wake up the next morning and make pancakes. Taylor's stepfather makes pancakes sometimes, but her mother always tells her that she should thank her stepfather, and that takes away so much of the fun.

"Puke," Bobby says again. Taylor takes a right onto a side street so that she can pull over. Bobby leans his head out the window and pukes. Taylor is fairly sure that he has puked on the side of his car, but she just wants to get home at this point. He'll have to clean it up himself tomorrow. In the meantime, Taylor lets the engine idle and waits to see if Bobby pukes again.

***

During one of the driving lessons, Taylor's stepfather drove for the first part of the lesson. He drove her out to the country, and, like most times, he didn't say much. Taylor tried to keep an eye on him without looking directly at him. Partway out, Taylor realized that he could drive her out to the country, stop the car and rape her. She'd heard stories about girls getting beaten or raped by their stepfathers, and it was usually out in the country when somebody got killed in a horror film.

When Taylor's mom had just started dating her stepfather, her mom asked her what she thought about him. Taylor didn't say much. On the one had, with him around, she could get away with a little more, because he kept her mother busy. On the other hand, Taylor didn't really like him. There wasn't anything bad in particular, but they didn't talk to each other, and she couldn't picture talking to him about anything important or fun.

So when her stepfather got them out in the country, it seemed like it could be bad. Instead, he pulled into a gas station parking lot. It didn't seem like a place he'd take her to do something bad to her. When they came to a stop, he unbuckled his seatbelt and looked over at her. He was smiling. "Let's get you on the freeway today."

He had taken her out into the country so that she could have an

130

empty stretch of freeway to go on. Looking at him, Taylor realized that the thought that he could have done something to her hadn't even been in his head. He hadn't even thought about whether or not she'd be worried about what he was going to do to her.

***

Bobby did puke a second time. He pulled himself up a little and leaned hard out the window. Taylor could tell when he was done, because he slumped back in his seat and moaned quietly. She put the car in drive and headed to the corner, taking three right turns to get back onto the main street. Bobby rolls a little side to side in his seat. Taylor puts the stereo on, not even really paying attention to what's playing. Since it's Bobby's car, it's a hip-hop CD. She thinks it's Eminem, though she doesn't know what album.

The rest of the ride is fairly quiet. Bobby starts to slouch and quiet down. Taylor makes sure that she goes no more than four miles over the speed limit, like her stepfather told her. When she gets close to Bobby's house, she's not sure how to handle it. She slows down and pulls over a little away from the house. The front light is on, but the upstairs lights look like they're off, so it's possible that Bobby's parents are asleep. It's also possible that they turned the lights off so that they could watch a movie like in the theater. "Bobby," Taylor says.

Bobby doesn't quite moan. He doesn't really say anything. Taylor slaps his arm. "Bobby," she says again. "You need to get in your house."

Taylor looks at Bobby. She thinks about leaving him in the car and walking home. It's not that far a trip, but it's late, and she'd rather not be out alone at this time of night. Also, she isn't sure what she would do with the keys. She couldn't leave the keys in the ignition, but it didn't seem like a good idea to take them with her, either.

***

Taylor has heard her mother and her stepfather having sex before. It's always weird, and not just because it's always weird to hear or think about your parents having sex. It's especially weird to think about her stepfather having sex with anyone. His seriousness makes it hard to imagine him just wanting to make out or screw or drink. So she was a little surprised the first time that she heard them having sex. Or, she heard her mom. She couldn't tell if her stepfather was just quiet or if he didn't make any noise during sex. She'd listened for less than a minute, and then she went into her room and started texting her friends. She got into a fight with one of them because of something she'd sent, and she thought that it might have been because she was too freaked out from listening.

***

Taylor is listening to Bobby snore. It makes her wonder why anyone gets married anymore. Not that Bobby's a bad guy. He's actually a really good boyfriend most of the time, like when he buys her ice cream, or when he does his impression of Mr. Larson, the chemistry teacher. It's just that he never says that he's sorry for nights like tonight.

Taylor's heard her mother and her stepfather fight. Not too loud or too long, but not fighting seems like its own problem, too. If you

132

don't argue, then it seems like you must be too old and too tired to really be in love. But Taylor realizes, too, that she probably won't argue much with Bobby later.

Taylor sighs. This isn't a good weekend, but the next one will probably be better. They're supposed to be going to some park where they can hike. Being out in the woods means that Bobby will make out with her, which is all right. And it also means that, if they bring booze, it'll have to be shared with the group, so things will probably be okay. But tonight, she still needs to figure out what to do. None of the lights have come on in Bobby's house, but she can't let the car run for too long. She'll run out of gas, and maybe she'll die of carbon monoxide poisoning. She thinks that her stepfather mentioned that to her one day. Just talking about all the different dangers of cars. But Taylor can't totally be sure. She might not have been listening, but, even if she had been, that wouldn't help her now. Now, she has to figure out what to do.

Their Own Personal Judgment Day

As soon as Cody and Jaclyn saw the baby sleeper standing in their doorway, they recognized him from that psychic show where that cult leader had been shot. Maybe it really hadn't been a cult. His movement or group was something that Cody and Jaclyn had never heard of before.

Jaclyn had always been kind of torn on psychics, finding them hard to really take seriously when they were giving readings or whatever, but also feeling like she'd be jinxing herself if she ever said out loud that they were bullshit. The baby sleeper's appearance made him look kind of mystic or mysterious. It was like Mr. Salty had been given a shriveled apple for a head. Cody and Jaclyn let him in anyway, knowing that this man would be cradling their child tonight. That's what they'd brought him in for.

"Hello," said Cody, stepping back from the door to let him into their apartment. Emma, their daughter, was rolling around the floor in her little walker. She had a few cereal puffs on the table, but most of them had been crushed to pieces with the hard head of a Barney figure. Elmo was her favorite, but Barney would do in a pinch, and Jaclyn refused to give her a doll with long fur or hair while she was eating. Because Emma used him to smash her puffs so often, the dark parts of Barnie's eyes were beginning to get scraped off.

The baby sleeper didn't really look around, he just smiled at Emma. When he spoke, his voice was high and wheezy, not what they'd expected. "Howdy," was all the baby sleeper said. He'd never spoken on that psychic show or in any interview. The only one who'd really talked to the press was the one-eyed man who tried to tell the future entirely in Star Wars quotes. Cody had told Jaclyn a number of times that he hated that psychic, because he was almost certain that the psychic made up a bunch of the quotes. Jaclyn hadn't watched the Star Wars movies enough to have an opinion But she did kind of like having this guy in her apartment. He took enough steps for Cody to close the door, then he smiled down at Emma. Jaclyn said, "That's a very nice suit to be wearing to bed with a baby."

"It'll be fine," he rasped. He was, in fact, wearing a nice, pin-stripe suit. Jaclyn's grandfather might've worn it to a funeral or wedding. She couldn't imagine Cody wearing a suit like that unless it was for Halloween or a theme party. The suit was a little rum-pled, but that might've just been from his line of work. It occurred to Jaclyn that he might have already helped some other babies to a sound, peaceful sleep that same day, or maybe Emma was the first of a few he'd help that evening. The parenting books had indicated that seven or eight for a bedtime wasn't unusual, but that it was hard to come up with a standard for all infants. Maybe even busier parents kept their infants up later so that they could spend more time with them. That made Jaclyn wonder if there were enough sleepless babies in the city for this guy to rely only on his baby sleeping business. She supposed that, if he'd been on the psychic show, he must've had other things going. The one-eyed Star Wars psychic had regularly told the cameras how he could help people track their major life decisions, always closing by saying, "And that is not a Jedi mind trick." Jaclyn was pretty sure that the show where the guy had been assassinated had said what each psychic had done, like palm reading or helping the police find murderers or rapists. One said that she used her power to communicate with pets struggling with trans-species anxieties. Jaclyn blanked on what the baby sleeper's specialty was, but she was sure that it wasn't "baby sleeping". That might've been too hard to explain with their little, ten-second introductions.

"I like to dress professionally," he said. It didn't seem like he was joking as he said it, but Jaclyn felt like she was being made fun of for some reason. Or maybe like he was too much in control. It was possible, she supposed, that all of psychic work was just intimidation or tricking people. Maybe that's why a psychic would be a natural cult leader.

Jaclyn and Cody watched him until it got too awkward. "This is Emma," said Cody, gesturing towards their daughter. The baby sleeper nodded. He'd been recommended by a co-worker of Jaclyn's. Cody remembered her name as Pauline or Colleen or something. It was actually Patricia. In her office, Jaclyn had more co-workers with kids than Cody did at the PR firm. Jaclyn had been complaining about the sleepless nights Emma had been giving them, and the co-worker told her about this tall, spindly man who got paid to help put babies to sleep. This conversation was before the assassination on the psychic show had taken place, so there was no way to tip Jaclyn off that it would be someone she'd recognize.

"She cry, squirm, or just run around all night?" the baby sleeper asked.

Cody and Jaclyn looked at each other, and then Jaclyn said, "Run around. Crawl around, I guess. She won't lie down for anything. She'll just sit up in bed and sing or yell."

"She'll cry eventually," said Cody.

The baby sleeper nodded. "Seen it before," he said. "Is this when you want her to go to bed?"

Cody and Jaclyn looked at each other again. Jaclyn said, "Maybe another half hour. If that's okay."

The man nodded. Cody went to the kitchen, "Can I get you something?" he asked.

"Nah," he said, almost a whimper.

"May I sit down?"

Jaclyn showed him to the couch, and he took out a book and began to read. She didn't look at the title. Jaclyn wondered if the baby sleeper could tell that they'd watched the clip of the cult leader being murdered several times. Cody came back in with a glass of water, which he put on the table without taking a sip. Jaclyn and Cody played with their daughter, but in a self-conscious way that wasn't really fun for anyone. Playing peek-a-boo and singing too loud. Trying to get her to bop along with classic songs like "This Old Man" or "Row Your Boat" instead of TV theme shows. Little Emma would play along now and then, but, for the most part, she'd stare at them then peek at the baby sleeper. Emma didn't seem creeped out. Kids didn't know not to take things in stride, Jaclyn thought. She wondered at what age people lose that. The whole time, the baby sleeper might've looked at them once, though maybe he'd just been stifling a sneeze.

After exactly 30 minutes of reading, the baby sleeper put the book back in his briefcase and stood. "I'd like to pick her up now."

Neither Jaclyn nor Cody said anything. The baby sleeper nodded and picked Emma up out of her walker. She gurgled. "Pacifier?" the baby sleeper asked. They both stood for a few seconds before Jaclyn went to Emma's room and got her green pacifier. She realized that she could've gotten the blue one out of her purse in the living room, but she was used to having them all move into the bedroom together. When she came back, Emma had already put her head on the baby sleeper's shoulder. He smiled at Jaclyn. "You can do the honors," he said in that weak little voice of his. Jaclyn admitted to herself that she resented this man, even if he let her and Cody get a good night's sleep from now on. Jaclyn had to work to poke the pacifier into Emma's mouth. When she finally took it in, Emma closed her eyes and rubbed her cheek against the shoulder of the man's pinstripe suit. In Emma's defense, it did look soft. "Won't be long," he said. "Which room?"

Jaclyn sulked to their breakfast bar, and Cody led the baby sleeper to Emma's room. He came back looking at the floor. The hardwood had looked stylish and easy to clean when they'd first rented this place. And it was nice that it was easy for Emma to scooch along in her walker, but Jaclyn also knew it would mean more bruises when Emma was really learning to walk. It's hard to think of those things too far ahead.

Jaclyn brought Cody a glass of wine, and he kissed her on the neck. Jaclyn felt a little too numb to let anything really happen. Besides, who knew when the baby sleeper would come out. She led Cody to the table, where they sat. How that zombie-looking man could help a child sleep was beyond her. He seemed nice, but, still, she didn't care for the thought of anyone being in the bedroom with her child. Alone and in the dark. She put her hand on Cody's knee for just a few seconds and then looked away. It struck Jaclyn that a big event, like some guy getting gunned down live on TV, and all the fallout for the cult members that came after that, could sit in the air without really impacting her life. She talked about religion a little more now, but she still didn't go to church, and she didn't read or even own a bible, but the day-to-day things like Emma's not sleeping made them look for help. It made them feel like there was no control in the world. She looked around their apartment, seeing a couple of dolls and her Elmo book lying on the floor. She knew she should be picking them up, but she was too tired and tense to really do it at the moment.

They didn't speak until the baby sleeper came back, smiling. "She's out," he said. "Give it a few days. If she's not out at about this time regularly from now on, call me, and it should only take one more visit."

They stared at him for a while more. As they were writing him a check, Jaclyn asked, "So you were there when that guy got shot?"

Cody followed up immediately with, "Was he crazy, or was he all right?"

The baby sleeper stared at the check for a long time without flipping it over to look at the amount or the signature. His face was a weird mix of immobile and jiggly, which made it really hard to gauge his reaction. Cody said, "I mean, some of the papers say he was bad, but nobody's ever said what exactly he did. No real accusation was made, but he was gunned down."

The baby sleeper laughed or coughed or something. He rubbed the sagging tip of his nose and sighed. "I can't really answer that for you. But I'll tell you a story."

Cody looked over at Jaclyn. He probably was hoping she'd think of a way to cut this response off, but Jaclyn liked these weird little details that she could use for gossip at the office. Since Emma was born, there weren't a lot of new stories that her co-workers got into. A lot of what she had to say revolved around diapers and spit up, and they'd all been through that already. She wasn't sure what would get this guy to be quiet anyway. He was good at what he did, apparently, and that always intimidated Jaclyn a little. Or maybe she felt a little superstitious about alienating someone who'd just been so close to their child. She loved Emma, but Emma hadn't been what Jaclyn had expected.

"Years and years ago, there was this tiny little town someplace in Europe. In the mountains where outsiders generally didn't go looking. As often happens in these places, they developed their own idiosyncratic system of beliefs. They believed that God judged you on the very last day of your life, the day you died. Everyone got his or her own little Judgment Day."

Cody interrupted to ask if the baby sleeper wanted some wine. He made a face and shook his head, then continued. Jaclyn found herself hoping that the baby sleeper had earned his face through a lifetime of drinking. "So they eventually agreed to kill anyone who'd just done something really great. As a favor. To get them into heaven."

Jaclyn chuckled, but Cody shot her a glance. The baby sleeper kind of rolled his eyes, though it was hard to see under his drooping face. "If someone saved a family from a burning building, that family would thank him by inviting him to dinner and pouring him a big glass of wine and hemlock. If a family was broke, a widow with a good year of crops would give them food so that they'd drown her in their bathtub."

"Wouldn't that send them to hell?" Cody asked.

The baby sleeper smiled broadly, which was actually much less pleasant than when he made the face in response to the offer of wine. "Not in their beliefs. For them, as long as they did something nice on their last day, they'd go to heaven, too. It's crazy what people will let happen to feel peace of mind."

Cody rubbed his eyes. Jaclyn felt a little that way, too, but not entirely. Even if it was a lie, this story was something she could carry with her.

"It actually worked pretty well in their community, too. Everyone got along, and people would do amazingly nice things for each other, believing that they'd get killed and then sent on for an eternal reward. It wasn't until a new governing figure took over nearby lands at the foot of the mountains that things went downhill. Wanting to increase the size of its kingdom, some soldiers of this government infiltrated the town. When the practice of killing as a reward was discovered, the townspeople were branded savages and madmen. The whole town was burned to the ground. 'Perhaps you'll all go to heaven. Or to hell,' the soldiers said."

Jaclyn and Cody stared at him for a little bit. Cody drained his wine and went to pour another glass. "So what are you saying?" Jaclyn asked.

The baby sleeper let out the hint of a smile and then raised his hands in mock defense. "That's for you to figure out." After a pause, he added, "Maybe it's not the thing, maybe it's what it does that really matters, and thinking too much actually makes it worse."

Cody stood up. "You've done a nice thing today, helping us out. Maybe we should kill you instead of giving you a check."

The baby sleeper laughed. "I haven't been that nice. I don't think I've ever been that nice my whole life. And I'm just the thing, anyway."

Jaclyn touched Cody's hand. "Cody," she said, "we hired him to do this."

Cody shook his head and left the room. The baby sleeper raised his eyebrows, then let them fall. It was a long trip. "I'm sure your husband's not always like that," the baby sleeper said.

"No," said Jaclyn. "He really isn't."

"That's fine," he said. Then, he took the flower out of his lapel and gave it to Jaclyn. Set it in front of her on the table, anyway. She smiled without saying anything. "Well, get good sleep." The man took the check, folded it once, and slid it into his breast pocket without checking the amount. After he left, Jaclyn didn't get up to lock the door. She did watch it, though. She kept expecting the doorknob to start moving, for some reason. She thought about what she'd tell her co-workers. She'd never talked about the possibility that she'd seen Matthew Broderick. Not to them anyway. Cody didn't have a comment on her story when she'd told him.

And maybe nobody looks like they do in the movies and on TV. When Cody came back, nearly twenty minutes later, he said, "That guy creeped me out."

Jaclyn nodded and picked up the flower. "We should get some sleep," she said.

Cody agreed. She went to the garbage and tossed in the flower, then she brushed her teeth and crawled into bed next to Cody. They listened to the hum of the air conditioning, not hearing anything else. It was supposed to make them comfortable in all weather. Jaclyn rolled onto her side, away from Cody, and she thought about watching the footage of that guy getting killed. The guests, the other psychics, just seemed flat, except for the supposedly gifted psychic host of the show, who fell to his knees and was screaming for them to go to commercial. There was something personal, something inaccessible going on. As she thought about all this, Jaclyn felt like she should probably be crying or something, but nothing really clicked. She sighed and considered trying to get Cody to have sex with her as a little celebration of Emma sleeping, but that'd just keep her up longer, and she really wasn't in the mood. So, she closed her eyes and counted backward from 200, hoping she wouldn't reach zero.

Supposedly Impervious to Fire

Looking back, I think my cousin tried to fall so much because it was so slapsticky, like the Three Stooges. That made it a better hobby than something serious like karate or coin collecting. He'd always roll his eyes or pretend to stumble around after he stood back up, making it a joke. Or he'd shake his head and make that noise like Sylvester the cat or some other cartoon character. It was part of fucking with his dad, I think. The Three Stooges thing, I mean. My cousin, Shawnie, hated his dad, so being like the Three Stooges was a good way to show him what an idiot he was. Or maybe he just liked the Three Stooges. I never totally got Shawnie. I never hated my father like Shawnie hated his. But Shawnie wasn't just about anger. He had focus, building up from falling off the swingset to dropping from the top of the jungle gym to jumping off the shed's roof to falling out of a second-story window. When I think about it, it's weird that he's even alive anymore. But we all got used to it pretty quickly, which I guess is weird, too.

In all fairness, I didn't see my cousins all that often, so when Shawnie would come to the reunion with a gouge on his face from the picket fence, or a black eye from hitting the woodpile, it made sense. Usually, we'd hear it from Shawnie's mom after a couple of beers, but everyone in Shawnie's family told us about the second-floor window incident. His mom, his dad and his sister all told it the exact same way. They all agreed that it was a second-floor window and that Shawnie shook for about three minutes straight after he fell. Even with his craziness, Shawnie was, in his way, safer than the older cousins like James and Todd. James was a nice enough guy, maybe, but Todd especially scared me. He might've been the big reason I hated the reunions.

For the '87 reunion, we were at my uncle Eddie's, and my brother and Todd and maybe a couple of younger cousins were down at the point, a sort-of peninsula that had all kinds of spiders and bugs crawling around. The water had frogs and sometimes crayfish. Then there was always a bunch of rocks and fallen trees that gave us lots of things to flip over, and there were always beetles or salamanders or other things underneath. Something to chase the girl cousins around with. The point was also close enough to the reunion itself to be safe, but far enough away that you could get into the kind of trouble you might want to at a family reunion. Throwing rocks at fragile things if you were young, and smoking pot (I think that's as hard as it got for Todd at the reunions) if you were old. Though if Todd had smoked a little more pot, maybe he would've been more sleepy and less cruel.

That year, Todd put a salamander down my oldest girl cousin's back. For some reason, the first 7 of us were boys, and then were a few girls, then an even mix. Maybe the girls caught more shit because there were so many older boys. Either way, this poor, girl cousin really got hosed that reunion. She screamed and ran away, which was probably the best thing for her to do. Todd laughed, and then he turned to my brother and me. My brother started laughing, but I said, "Salamanders are supposed to be impervious to fire," which was really stupid.

Todd's laughter stopped, but he kept smiling. He asked, "Do you know what 'impervious' means?"

Even at 10 or 11, I knew Todd's full attention was bad news, so I just shook my head and looked out at the water. There wasn't a cloud in the sky. Way off in the distance was a fishing boat with what was probably two guys with a case of beer and not much interest in catching fish. "Invulnerable," said Todd, punching my arm.

I said, "Ow," and he called me a pussy, then walked off, laughing. I rubbed my arm, and my brother punched me in the same spot on the other arm. "Ow," I said again, but I got it. "For balance," my brother told me. I picked up a really small rock and threw it at him. Because we'd just been playing with Todd, I said, "Dick".

My brother dodged the rock without really having to try, but his eyes got really wide. He yelled, "I'm telling Mom and Dad". Then he left, too. So I was alone at the point. The other cousins had taken off after Todd put the salamander down the oldest girl's back. I kicked at the grass as I walked around a bit, and then I saw a garter snake that was eating a frog. This was on the way back from the point, on this stretch of land that had a lot of trees and only a little bit of path. I don't know why the snake wasn't more back in the woods. It looked really cool at first, all the blood and guts and slime, exactly what a boy would want to see. But it just seemed boring after a while. The frog wasn't really kicking, but I wondered what made it die. Was it blood loss? Suffocation? I decided that I'd head back towards my uncle's house to get some of those jelly fruits that are coated with sugar. I always ate them in a specific sequence, orange, red, purple, green, always leaving yellow for my dumber cousins who would eat anything.

When I got back to the deck, I got some jelly fruit and asked one of my aunts, "How come there's no blue fruit?"

She sipped a clear drink out of her clear cup, which had little plastic fruit floating in between the inside and outside of the glass. "Because there is no blue fruit," she said. Her husband, my uncle by blood, looked at my shirt, which was blue except for the bat signal on it, and said, "Are you a blue fruit?"

I laughed and just said, "No," but she called him by his first name, which, even then, I knew meant that he'd done something bad, like when parents call you by your whole name. My uncle grabbed a handful of nuts, another beer, and then he walked off. Probably, you could almost always say that that uncle grabbed a handful of nuts, another beer, and then walked off. My aunt said, "How old are you, now?" I think I told her whatever my age was. I had no reason to lie, but that doesn't mean that I didn't. She must've seen asking me as enough of an apology for my uncle, because she just said, "That's nice," and went off to talk to another adult, which was fine by me. She had ugly hair, and I don't think she actually liked kids, even though she had two of them. I never really talked to them, and they usually only played with each other. I looked around at the table with all the food. There was a lot of stuff, and the trick for the reunion was always to find junk food that we didn't have at home. Doritos were, of course, delicious, but the wiser approach was to fill up on Aunt Debbie's peanut butter and fudge bars, which my mom never made. By that time, though, they were all mushy and ugly in the hot sun, so I ate my candy fruit and grabbed a handful of mixed nuts, careful to sift out the Brazil nuts and grab some extra cashews. They didn't go well with the candy. I saw my mom looking at me, which meant that my brother probably had told her that I'd said a bad word. Or that I'd thrown a rock. I started walking away from the deck to see how long I could go without getting yelled at.

It was just a little after I slunk away that the fighting started. First, it was Todd's dad yelling at him. I didn't see all of it, but I remember watching him hit Todd once in the ear and once in the head, then he took a drag off his cigarette. Todd started rubbing his ear, and his dad slapped him on the back of the head. Todd said, "Fuck". His dad looked at him, but he didn't hit him anymore. Maybe he'd noticed that a lot of the family was watching him. Todd and his dad wandered to different parts of the woods. I went to where the sodas were. This was more towards the house, and my oldest girl cousin was playing with the same toy horse that she always was. A light tan thing with plastic bows in its stupid mane. The tail was broken off. I wasn't close enough to my cousin to care that much, but it was still a little sad. I didn't want her to have shitty toys.

I watched her for a minute. She galloped the horse across the ground, then in the air, then on the ground again. "Todd's dad really walloped him," I said, using a word my own dad would've said. I watched her spin her horse. "Todd's dad is always hitting him," she said. I didn't know what to say to that. She was right, for sure.

"I'm sorry he put the salamander down your back," I said.

She flipped her horse in the air and caught it easily, "All the root beer is gone."

I was surprised. I guess, though, any kid would know the root beer was gone, and I think it was the only flavor that was gone. This cousin was from the branch of the family that always looked a little bit dirty to me. I even caught, now and then, that she'd be wearing my clothes as a hand me down. That could've been that her parents really didn't care, and it could've just been her being a tomboy or, like her brother Shawnie, trying to annoy her father. He wouldn't have liked her being a lesbian, and I know a tomboy isn't a lesbian, but her dad wouldn't have. Either way, it made me feel bad, but not in a way that I would've talked to her about. "I bet a horse could crush a snake, because its hooves are so big and heavy," I said.

She pulled the horse close to her. "A horse wouldn't notice the snake, dummy."

I sighed loud, being a kid trying to be subtle. I looked around and thought about wandering off, but having her insult me was still better than bumping into Todd, especially out in the woods. I picked up a pinecone, but it was full of pitch, and I tossed it away. I tried to pick some grass to wipe the pitch off my fingers, but that just left a bunch of grass on my hands. I was about to walk off, thinking that I might as well go let my mom yell at me, when Todd came over. He looked down at my cousin, who started to hug her horse even tighter. "Did you know horses eat their own shit?" he asked.

My cousin said, "No they don't," and stuck her tongue out.

Todd looked at me, then back at her. "Would you eat a horse's shit?"

She scooted back a little on her knees, but she didn't get up. "You would," she said to Todd.

Todd picked up what I was pretty sure was the same pine cone I'd tossed away, but he picked it up by the little stem so that he didn't get anything on his fingers, which made me hate him that much more. Then, he moved a little closer to her. I had no idea what he was going to do, and I might have even been a little curious to see what you can actually do to a person with a pinecone anyway, but I said, "Leave her alone," and then took three steps back, hoping that I could run away before he would do something to me. Actually, I kind of hoped he'd chase my other cousin. Instead, he looked down at the pinecone. It sucked, watching him make a decision about some mean and stupid punishment involving a pinecone. But that's when Shawnie walked by. His hair was standing up in back, and there was the beginning of a tear around the collar of his shirt. It wasn't one of mine. Todd looked over and smiled. "Shawnie," he said.

Shawnie burped. Todd nodded and held up the pinecone. "Do you want to eat this?"

Shawnie shrugged. "How much will you give me?" he asked.

Todd looked at the pinecone. "It's not that big." He tilted it to look at it from the bottom. "You can eat the whole thing and I'll give you a quarter, or you just eat the pitch and then I won't break your sister's stupid pony."

"Let me see it," Shawnie said. His sister was starting to relax, which seemed weird to me. I thought she and Shawnie hated each other, and that Shawnie would walk off and laugh when Todd grabbed the pony. But maybe this was more about proving himself as a man than it was about him crapping on his sister. Maybe hating was caring for Shawnie. Todd handed him the pinecone and

Shawnie looked at it, then sniffed it. He shook his head. "This kind is poison."

Todd rolled his eyes. "Christ, you would say that."

Shawnie shrugged again. "If I die, your dad's really going to beat you."

I watched his face, to see if Shawnie knew that this was the wrong thing to say. It seemed like he'd have to, but he didn't show any kind of fear, regret or any other sign of common sense. The weird thing, though, is that Todd didn't even reply. He must've been pissed after his dad punched him before, but he didn't say anything. It was like watching some dingbat civilian outfox all of Cobra's secret military installation while GI Joe looked on. "Okay," said Todd. "I'm going to hit one of these dickwads in the back of the head. Do you want it to be your sister or the other one?"

Shawnie frowned like he was actually thinking. He looked at me, "the other one", then at his sister. After watching him sort of stick up for his sister, I thought maybe he'd stick with that and ask Todd to hit me. I didn't have any reason to think that Shawnie liked me or even remembered that we were related. But Shawnie looked back at the pinecone. "Well," he said, "I'll make you a deal. If you eat this pinecone and don't die, then I'll let you whack my sister over the head with any branch you want, and I'll take the blame."

Todd squinted. I assumed that he was trying to figure out whether or not he was being scammed, and, to be honest, I had no idea either. After a couple of seconds, Shawnie said, "You can't shit your pants or puke everything up, either." I think that was the genius part, though I can't really explain why.

Todd muttered, "You're so fucking weird," and walked off. As he did, he grabbed the pinecone from Shawnie and threw it at me. I was able to dodge it, but I knew I looked like a girl when I did, and Todd laughed.

We all sat or stood very quietly for a few seconds. "That was cool," I told Shawnie. He knelt down, watching me the whole time, picked up a new pinecone, and put it in his mouth. It made me wonder how the pitch would taste. Not enough to try it, of course, but I knew, even then, that there was fundamental difference between Shawnie and me. He was Batman, and he'd just stared down the Joker. Well, the Penguin, maybe. I said, "Thanks, Shawnie", and walked away. As soon as I turned my back, I heard a sound and felt something hit the back of my head. I turned around and Shawnie was smiling. "Jerk," I said, and I walked away. I ran my hand over the back of my head and felt a little bit of pitch in my hair, though I might've put it in there my own self from the stuff that was in my fingers before.

The upshot of it all was that my parents yelled at me for calling my brother a dick and for having pitch in my hair, but I was at least able to wash the pitch off my hands with a wet can of cream soda, which was okay, but not a real substitute to root beer. Lucky for me, my brother tried to set a small tree on fire a little later in the reunion. Even though he didn't come close to doing it, he still got yelled at. It was a family reunion, so there was always someone yelling at someone. One of my cousins told me that Todd passed out in the woods, or maybe that was a different year.

And that's almost the end of it. But there was one last thing. As everyone was getting into their cars at the end of the day, I was watching Shawnie. Todd had steered clear of him the whole rest of the reunion, passed out or not, which made it harder for him to be as intimidating at the rest of the reunions. He still was, but not like he had been.

But this is about Shawnie. While he was piling into his family's station wagon, he kind of slipped, and he fell back onto the driveway. I couldn't tell if his head hit or not, but he got up, brushed himself off and got back in without really reacting, and it made me wonder if he'd done it on purpose. And that's the thing that impressed me. Not that he'd fall, but that there was the possibility that he'd really fall and just take it in stride. Like he'd expected to happen, or that he'd fallen so often that he was totally used to it. And that must've been why he could take on Todd. Todd stumbled into his parents' car, eyes barely open. So did his dad, though his dad dropped into the seat behind the wheel. And he's still alive, too, for some reason.

And that was it for that reunion. It was about like any other reunion except for that one interaction. That pony and that pinecone. But maybe that was just for me, like the snake and the frog. Maybe every cousin had some breakthrough moment at one of the reunions. If I'd asked Shawnie about the pinecone, I'm sure that he would've just fucked with me, or maybe he wouldn't have even remembered.

When my little chunk of the family drove through all the woods, my brother and I listened to our parents tell us why we'd embarrassed them. I guess it's not that surprising, either. I put on headphones and listened to something and wondered which one of my cousins would be the first to die. It seemed like an obvious question to think about, after the reunion. All these years later, it's sort of surprising to see who it was. Or maybe not. I knew I wouldn't be one of the first, but that's not really a compliment to me, either. It's just not the worst possible insult.

The Kid Next Door

On Tuesday, the neighbors ask Justin to go into their apartment and threaten to eat their child if the kid won't stop playing with the Halloween decorations. It's not the first time. From what Cassie can remember, there's a fuzzy pumpkin face in particular that the kid keeps going for. Cassie thinks she remembers her family having about the same decoration from when she was a kid. The kid's name is Alex, she thinks. Or maybe Adam. Justin is okay with it this time and, through the wall, Cassie hears the kid crying and saying he won't touch it again. Then, she hears the low growl of Justin's monster voice. She shivers, wondering how this will shape Justin's approach to fatherhood. If they ever actually have kids. Maybe the two of them won't stay together, but moving in together seems like a big step to Cassie. She listens again.

Cassie thinks it should've been harder for the neighbors to talk Justin into this. It seemed funny at first. He'd told her how the wife had gone up to him and asked him for help. Told him their kid was already a little scared of him, which was weird, though Justin was tall and trying to grow a beard. It seemed like a bad sign. On the other hand, Justin has started using the monster voice in bed, and he's been more assertive once that started.

Cassie hears the slow trudge of Justin's monster, and she goes back to their apartment's dining area. For some reason, Justin doesn't like her to listen to him being the monster. Maybe he gets creeped out by the overlap of the kid he terrorizes and the woman he has sex with. Though that would be an issue if they had kids, too, maybe. Hopefully they'd never need a monster.

Tuesdays, Cassie and Justin have a four-hour window of time together, so they're having chicken, fettuccini Alfredo, and broccoli. A nice dinner that isn't super pricey. Most of the parts of the dinner are frozen, so Justin won't be stuck with too many dishes when Cassie goes to work. Justin will probably be asleep when she comes home.

The door opens. Cassie hears the normal Justin footsteps. "Make him cry?" Cassie asks. Justin wrinkles his face. "Scourge of little boys, savior of cardboard jack-o-lanterns."

"My hero." Cassie dips her broccoli in a little more sauce and puts it in her mouth. Justin sits at the table. "He'll grow up to be a good boy who listens."

Cassie nods. "Until he builds a monster-killing cannon."

Justin laughs and eats some noodles, and Cassie wonders if she should've gone to the couch so they could watch TV while eating. Someday, they'll probably watch nothing but Sesame Street. Last night before they went to bed, they watched I Shouldn't Be Alive, and she talked to Justin about how glad that she was that they didn't live in the Southwest with all the scorpions and snakes. Justin told her that plenty of people lived in the Southwest without getting bitten, and plenty of people got bit without living in the Southwest. Cassie had asked if anyone in the Southwest ever died of monster attacks, and that had led to sex. That was fine, but Cassie did wonder if there could be any brown recluse spiders in their apartment. She was pretty sure they were even worse than black widows. Black widows were the most poisonous spider people talked about when Cassie was a kid. But they'd seemed far away. Brown recluses are supposed to live near them, or in their area, or however you'd say it. But she can't remember exactly where she would've heard that in the first place anyway.

***

Cassie and Justin are finishing their dinner without saying much. Justin does ask a little about work. Cassie doesn't mind her work, but she hates talking about it. It's only Thursday, and already the neighbors are asking for the monster again. Cassie thinks that they're turning into monster addicts. What will the psychological effect on Adam or Alex be? Or Justin, for that matter? And what if the monster's overall effect is wearing off? After all, how many times can the monster come over before the kid notices that the monster never does anything? As she thinks about this, Cassie realizes that she has no idea how old the boy is. She thinks about how hard it is for someone without kids to guess the age of a kid. What's their reference point?

The monster should strike tonight, though, because the kid really crossed a line. He hit Mommy and won't apologize. Even Cassie thinks this is a biggee. Justin is supposed to threaten not only to eat the kid, but to share him with a gorilla as well. There might also be a clown involved, but Cassie can't hear everything through the wall. Maybe she only thinks that because she hated clowns when she was young. Clowns and spiders and snakes. She hasn't yet heard spiders come up with the kid, but whatever they just said to the kid, he's crying now. Cassie wonders if the kid just had a hard day at school. Then she wonders what a hard day at school is for a kid who's whatever age Alex or Adam is. Did he get punched by a bully? Did he have to watch a video on clowns or spiders and get creeped out? Cassie goes back to the kitchen. She has to work again tonight, but she sneaks half a glass of wine. She doesn't think Justin will notice, and she knows that her dipshit manager won't. He once complimented that fucktowel Todd for his "excellent customer service" when Todd was just baked out of his mind. Maybe if Cassie went in a little tipsy, she'd get promoted for being so friendly. Then she wondered if maybe their manager comes in to work drunk. He spends most of his time in his office. Cassie sighs; the wine wasn't even that good.

Cassie and Justin aren't at a point in their lives where they'd buy good wine, and, to be honest, she doesn't think she'd know the difference anyway. But she knows this wine isn't great, so she drains it, rinses the glass and puts the glass in the strainer. She starts to go back to the wall, but before she gets there, she hears Justin coming back, so she walks back to the couch, where she sits down and tries to look sober. She turns on the TV and is at least flipping channels. I Shouldn't Be Alive is on again, but Cassie isn't feeling up to it today. Justin comes in and walks to the couch, but doesn't sit down. Cassie keeps flipping and she starts to wonder if she's breathing too loudly. Then she realizes that Justin wants her to ask him about Adam or Anthony or whatever. "Did you have to nibble on him at all today?"

Justin chuckles, then sits down. "Sometimes, I feel bad when

I see him in the hall. It's like, I never feel bad when I'm called in to scare him, because he's done something that makes his parents want me in there, but when we're just passing in the hall, maybe I'm ruining his day for no good reason, because he thinks that the monster could get him at any time and for no reason."

Cassie shrugs and pauses on some stupid show about stupid people. "He probably did something bad every day so maybe he feels bad about whatever he did." Justin slumps on his couch. "Is this what we're watching?"

Cassie starts flipping again. "I thought we were talking, so I stopped." The History Channel was something about the Deadly Sins, so Cassie stops on that. The guy on the TV is talking about how lust was compartmentalized in men's lives in Ancient Greece. "Do you want the remote?" Cassie asked.

Justin shakes his head. "Weekend tomorrow."

"Yep." Now the show has some etching of this creepy guy leering. It's supposed to be a god or a demon or something, but it looks like a clown to Cassie. One of the girls she and Justin went to high school with claimed that she had sex with some TV clown. In makeup. Cassie never believed her.

"The parents said they're going to that orchard out by Highway 8 to pick apples and drink cider."

"Do you want kids?" she asks.

Justin stares at the TV, then he shrugs. Cassie looks at the time on the cable box and sees she'll have to leave in an hour, which means she'll have to start getting ready in less than a half hour, which means that Justin probably could wait her out. Cassie wonders if the etchings of anger would look like a clown or a monster. Then she wonders what monsters looked like in the dark ages. She knows that the etchings weren't from the dark ages, but she doesn't know exactly when they'd be from. She's just thinking about monsters before special effects and really good costumes.

"When I was little," Justin starts, "my brother and I stayed overnight at our aunt's house. They didn't say why when they dropped us off. It was the only time that we spent the night there. It wasn't until I grew up that I realized my mom was letting my aunt test drive parenthood."

Cassie looks at the clock again. "Well, you guys do have cousins, right?"

Justin touches Cassie on her knee. "If we wanted to test drive, like going to the orchard, that's out of the question for me."

Cassie puts her hand over Justin's. "Justin, would the neighbors really let us test drive their kid?"

Justin's hand loosens. "Why wouldn't they?"

"We're not family." Cassie puts the volume three notches lower.

"They let me in their home to scare their child."

Cassie looks at the TV and wonders if she could wait this out. There's another bearded old man talking about how lust used to be. Cassie doesn't know if it's the wine or something else, but her cheeks feel hot. "We don't really talk to them much. They only picked you because you're their tallest neighbor."

Justin says, "Never mind, I guess." There's something about apples on the TV, and Cassie regrets having the wine.

***

Cassie and Justin are at home when the neighbors come back from what must've been a very bad trip to the orchard. The little boy's screaming at the parents, and they don't seem to be answering back at all. Cassie and Justin are eating chips on the couch, and she touches his arm. "Don't go. They're just using you."

Justin smiles. "Maybe they won't even ask."

Cassie swirls the chips in the bowl. "If they do?"

Justin's bottom lip tugs a little. It never occurred to her before, but she thinks, now, that Justin would probably choose their kids over her, and she knows she'd resent it a little, though maybe being a mother would change that. "Let's be quiet, and maybe they won't even knock."

Cassie puts the bowl of chips on their coffee table, then she lays back on the couch, laying her lags over Justin's lap. He laughs a little and swats her knee. She rubs her legs up and down his, and he pinches her thigh. Soon, she's sitting on his lap and sliding her hands up his chest. "Oh Mr. Monster," Cassie says. "What sexy fur you have." They kiss, and Cassie can hear the neighbors yelling, then their front door opens. Before the knock comes, she starts to moan. Justin grabs her arm and shakes his head. Cassie looks at him and waits for the knock, which hasn't come yet. She kisses Justin's neck, but he shakes his head again. Cassie slides off his lap and back onto the couch, and she moans again a little louder this time. Justin leans towards her and hisses, "stop it." The feet in the hall scurry away, and Cassie wonders if it was the mom. She wonders if the dad would've stayed to listen for a while. He has long hair and a gut. He looks like the type who would listen. Cassie thinks that she'd crack up if she was having sex while someone was listening. Justin's never really talked about fetishes or anything. The monster voice is as far as they've gone, which is fine.

Cassie looks at Justin, who turns on the TV and flips to a dumb action movie. The kind they show on basic cable. Next door, the parent (it is the mom's voice) says something, and the kid's yelling stops, then turns to crying. Cassie wonders if the mom told the kid that the monster got killed by a clown that was even meaner and scarier than the monster. Or a gorilla clown or a spider clown. Then Cassie tells herself that she should grow up. She sighs, pats Justin's leg and mouths "sorry". He nods and turns back to the action movie. There's not even a big muscley star in this one. The hero just looks like a guy. Cassie would like to get up. She'd like to go shower, or drink or take a nap. But if she leaves now, Justin will be pouty most of the day, so she picks up the chips and watches the plain guy get his revenge. She thinks it's stupid. Who'd be scared of this plain guy, no matter how big a gun he has. "Do you want something to drink?" she asks.

She knows he'll say yes, but she thinks he says it just to give her permission. She wonders what he'd do if she dropped to the floor and threw a tantrum. But she knows she wouldn't really know how to do it.

An Impulse Buy

The first sale was at this old lady's house. Not old like me, like my daughter tells me I'm old, but actually old. The kind of old lady that sits in a folding chair bundled in a jacket and sniffles. As far as I could tell, this lady was putting on the garage sale only to confirm her belief that humanity was not worth interacting with. She had a dented waffle maker for ten dollars and these bears that were mostly missing eyes and ears and that had been dumped into a cardboard box. It reminded me of the island of misfit toys from the old Rudolph movie, but like it had gone through the apocalypse.

It wouldn't have been so bad, but partway through my wife's exploration, this black lady came to the sale. She brought a blanket up to the old lady and asked how much it was. I picked up a laughing Santa from the misfit toy box and turned it around in my hands. The old lady looked her up and down and said, "What'll you give me?"

I wanted to call my wife over, because Susan's the kind of woman who would've stuck up for the poor black lady, but she was pretty far back in the old lady's garage, sorting through a stack of sweaters, which I suppose would've been the one thing that was good at that sale. There weren't any DVD's or books for me to look at, so I hadn't progressed past the knick knacks. I traded the laughing Santa for an Easter bunny that had most of the fake fur rubbed off. The black lady looked all around the blanket, maybe hoping that a price tag would turn up or maybe hoping that she could wait out the old lady and get an actual price. If it was the second, then the old lady won, because the black lady eventually said "Eight bucks?"

I waited to see if any slurs would come. The old lady rolled her eyes. I heard a car slow down, then drive on, having the good sense to not stop here. The black lady shifted her weight to one foot. She set the blanket on top of some old board games. "Well what do you want?" The old lady waved her hand, "Just take it, then."

I quickly looked back at the trinkets, desperately wanting to avoid getting sucked into the conversation. There was a sigh, then the black lady said, "Nevermind. You should price your stuff". It was a mild insult, but the old lady started to cough hard. It made me wonder how many people each year die just to spite someone else. Mercifully, Susan came back empty handed. "Let's go," she said, quietly. The old lady was still coughing when we got in the car.

At the next sale, Susan walked up to me holding a couple of nice shirts, both solid colors. "How much?" I asked.

"Dollar a piece," she said. I had no reason to get or even want them, but I also knew that saying, "no" would get on her nerves if I couldn't say why. And it was a good deal.

"Looks good," I said. Susan nodded, then showed me a purse that was only two dollars.

I nodded, and she looked at the table I was standing at. "Are you looking at wrestling figures?" she asked.

I did an impression of myself chuckling. "I was just surprised to see a toy that I played with when I was a kid."

She patted my gut. "That's quite a while ago all right, old man." I smiled at her, glad that she didn't suggest that I buy them. They were probably only a quarter a piece, as cheap as everything else was. Maybe a dime, even. I decided not to even check the price, but it also made me want to find something for my daughter, a doll or movie or book. I did a quick sweep of the sale with my eyes, but I pretty much knew my wife would've seen a toy worth getting if there had been one. Then again, maybe she was leaving something to help me out, to make me feel like I was part of this shopping expedition. "I'm going to look at the movies," I said.

"Okay," she said, refolding my shirts. I shuffled two tables down and checked what they had. A lot of sci-fi, the kind of stuff that I would've liked in middle school, but Leslie, our daughter, wouldn't have liked them. She was much more of a sword and sorcery kind of girl. Which is not sci-fi, I have come to find out. I like that about her. There was a bunch of John Hughes movies. As much as I enjoyed them, I couldn't really see myself watching them enough to justify actually buying them. Something about the 80's always gave me an uneasy feeling. I sighed and went to Susan. She raised her eyebrows, and I nodded. I paid with a five, and the lady gave me a single and a thank you. I nodded to her, a different nod than I'd given Susan. This one was more quick and straight. The lady handed the stuff to us in a plastic grocery bag. Some folks would give the bag to the husband, but this lady must've watched us, because she knew I always paid and my wife always carried things, unless there was furniture involved. My wife and I went back to the car.

From our talk before leaving for the sales this morning, I knew that Susan was at a crossroads. She could go to one sale in a nice subdivision where the rich folks were just looking to clean out their house, so they priced nice things reasonably, or she could check out two or three sales by our house that were hit or miss. Given the drive time and when her workday began, we couldn't do both. She studied the map and sighed. "Let's go to Running Deer Hills."

I started the car, and we set off. Running Deer Hills was fine with me. There was something exciting in the trickle-down quality of our purchases from the rich pricks in the nice subdivision. Also, the long drive gave us more time to just sit together. With our daughter, we didn't have that time as often as we once did. When we had a baby sitter, there was always this weird pressure to enjoy ourselves that could undercut a real sense of fun, like smiling for a wedding photo or sitting through a school recital when your kid wasn't onstage. Something about the comfortable tedium of the drive was just nice. As we drove to the sale, we passed this kid who was building something. It was hard to see what it was. Something red, was all I could see. Susan turned on the radio. She alternated between NPR and this station that played a lot of 70's and 80's music. NPR was the usual bits about debt and corruption, and the radio station was Motley Crue and then Led Zepplin. I don't mind Zepplin, but it was a little early in the morning.

The problem with the rich prick sale was that they were really pushing the golf angle. I've never played. It's a game that needs too much patience. Fishing's different, because you're sitting and drinking while you do it, but golf requires concentration, which defeats the purpose of the drinking angle, to me. Though maybe you get used to doing it drunk and can't golf sober. That's how my father was with baseball. He could always hit better after a couple of beers loosened him up. I tried to remember if my father was my age when he stopped playing in the neighborhood league, but the lady running the sale kept telling me about things they had at the golf course or country club or something. I gave enough of a performance to look like I was listening, or maybe she just didn't want to blow a potential sale by calling me out on zoning out.

Still, there was some good stuff. Some decorations that Susan liked, a couple of pieces of baby clothes for her sister, and even a Clapton greatest hits that I didn't really need, but didn't want to pass up for only fifty cents. It wasn't great, but it was nice. Sadly, though, nothing for Leslie. It felt like a lame morning of garage sales, which gets down pretty far into the lame barrel.

On the ride back, Susan began to fiddle with the radio again. We both hate morning talk radio. Too many stupid comments and obvious jokes. It's just the wrong kind of predictability. So she settled on some station that was playing Journey, which was fine. We talked a little about Leslie's upcoming science report. It was on mongooses. I thought it should be mongeese, but she'd corrected me on that. Susan said that she was surprised that Leslie was so interested in mongooses being able to kill snakes. As we kept going, we came up to the kid again. The thing he was building was a little bigger. It looked like what you'd have if you tried to build a UFO out of cardboard, duct tape and sticks. But he'd painted a bright red and yellow hero firing what was apparently a gun. I pulled over just a little way away from him. "Just a minute," I said, getting out of the car. Susan didn't have a direct response. "Hey kid," I said.

The kid looked up at me, giving me the stranger-danger once over. But he must've decided that I was harmless, because he stepped towards the thing he was building and said, "Yeah?"

I gestured towards the thing and asked, "How much?" I recognized that I was opening myself up to the same level (though certainly not the same type) of criticism that that poor black lady had.

The kid shrugged. "It's not really for sale."

"Really?" I said. I tried to stay back, not looking like I was working to intimidate him.

"It's mine," he said. I rubbed my chin with my knuckles. This was the invigorating stress that I was used to having from a child.

"You know," I said, if you sell it to me, you could probably buy a real one."

The kid squinted at me. "Do you even know what it is?"

I smiled. "Sure," I said.

Thankfully, he didn't ask me to say. He looked at the thing, then at me. "A hundred dollars," he said.

I nodded, then looked at it. "I'll give you ten," I said.

The kid frowned. "I get to keep the tape that I haven't used yet."

I tapped my chin again and made a show of walking around the thing, then I sighed. "All right," I said. "Deal." I stuck out my hand, and the kid kept eye contact with me as he took it and shook it. I took out my wallet and handed him ten dollars. He took it and ran off. After he was a ways off, I folded up the thing, trying carefully not to bend the cardboard. I put it into the back seat of my car, then got back into the driver's seat. My wife looked at it by looking in the rearview mirror. "What is it?" she asked.

I got the car back on the road before answering. "A real find," I said. She nodded and turned on the radio. Madonna was on as part of some kind of flashback Friday programming. "Like a Virgin." My wife left it on. I'm not a huge fan of Madonna, but, that morning, I really didn't mind.

No Running

Bryan could sort of recognize the family that he was watching in the pool. He recognized them in the way that he'd recognize any of the regulars or semi-regulars. Two parents and one kid, not much of a drowning risk. The dad was buzzcutty, but he didn't seem like a dick. Maybe just old-school. This family would sneak in a pool toy that they weren't supposed to have now and then, but they wouldn't argue with the other families, and they never tried to stay too late. Not like the white trash families or the kids he just knew would call him a prick if he chased them out. Bryan watched the dad toweling off, and looked towards the kid, still floating, bobbing up and down in his life jacket. The mom was halfway between the dad and the kid, and the dad was trying to flag the mother over. She was waving to the kid to swim towards her. "Come on," she kept saying.

The dad wiped himself down from his trunks to his shins. "If you get out, he'll start swimming". The dad sounded pretty sure of himself. It was possible, but Bryan didn't want to have to watch. Bryan looked towards the diving board. Some fat kid who always plugged his nose was bouncing a little. There was a youngish girl behind him that Bryan didn't recognize. Not that he recognized all the regulars. The young kids, Disney swimsuits and Waterwings, the middle-aged folks, hairy guts and dimpled asses and all that tended to blend together to him. But the girl in the faded red bikini who had a rose tattoo on the small of her back or the redhead whose bottom always rode up stood out for Bryan. So did the fat girl who was not nearly ashamed enough of her body.

The fat kid did what was actually a pretty decent dive off the board, and the little girl watched him paddle back to the side before she got towards the end of the board. She ended up doing a nice dive without much splash. Bryan wondered who her family was. When he looked back to the family with the little kid, he saw that the mom was closer to the side of the pool, but she had her back to the dad. Bryan chewed on his whistle a little. The kid was starting to cry. Not a full-on wail, but enough that he couldn't pretend not to notice. The mom was saying, "You can do it, Skipper." The dad was shaking his head. "You'll have to spend the night here, Buddy," he said. It wouldn't be long before Bryan would have to step in. Saving a kid for real was glamorous, but talking to parents was just a pain. He took the whistle out of his mouth and took a deep breath. At the side of the pool a MILF was putting a second coat of sunscreen onto her kid. The family had been at the pool for about half an hour, and the mom had sat in the sun the whole time.

Bryan looked down at his watch. It was still at least a half hour before anyone would come to replace him. And Jeff was replacing him, so it might be longer. Plus, he wasn't sure that letting a dick-head stoner like Jeff take on this family was a good idea anyway. Either way, he shouldn't try to just wait this out. "You'll like it," said the dad. "It'll be like sleeping in a waterbed. Like Aunt Claire."

The mom kind of yelled at the dad, and the kid cried more. Bryan couldn't tell if the dad got yelled at for teasing the kid or for bringing up Aunt Claire. Bryan blew his whistle and yelled, "No running" to no one in particular. He was disappointed that so few people looked to see if the whistle was for them.

When Bryan had first started, Lizzie, the manager that he'd really wanted to nail, had told him that wearing sunglasses was an easy way to make people believe you were watching them. She'd told him that people had guilty consciences, and the idea that they were being watched could actually be as good as watching them. At the time, Bryan had said, "Like in poker". Within half a minute, Bryan had started thinking of other things that he could've said to impress Lizzie enough to get her to sleep with him. But he was very glad for the tip about the sunglasses, and it had stopped some families from making trouble. That family with the Disney towels had folded very quickly. But that didn't make him layworthy to Lizzie.

It didn't help him right now, either. The mom started going to the kid, and the dad said, "He can make it." The dad looked over to Bryan. "Trying to teach him how to swim so he can pass out of the swim class he's in."

At two full summers, Bryan had enough experience to tell that when a parent, especially a father, stated the obvious, he was trying to get you on his side. It's like they thought that if you started off agreeing with them on the easy stuff, then maybe they could keep you going. Mothers would never do that. They'd usually try some kind of logic, and they'd giggle if they were good looking, which actually always worked. But only on the guy lifeguards. With this dad, Bryan thought he should've said, "Doesn't look like he's enjoying it," but instead he just said, "Yeah." In addition to this being Bryan's third summer, it would probably be his last, so his main goals were to not do so poorly that he couldn't ask for a reference for later job applications, and to get a few phone numbers so that he could get laid the rest of the summer and his final year of college. This whole kid issue wasn't going to help him out with either goal.

The mother was almost to the little boy when the dad said, "He can do it, Denise. Leave him be." Then, turning to Bryan, he said, "He'll move today. It's all a matter of motivation."

Bryan said nothing and looked towards the diving board. The fat kid was up again. He stomped his way down the board, bounced and executed a decent cannonball. There was a scrawny little kid waiting for him to swim. The kid had red hair, and he was very pale. The kind of kid who either burned badly or never really stopped being white the whole summer. Bryan glanced back at Skipper's family. The mother was at the ladder, and the kid had fallen into a quiet sob. Bryan looked over to where the slides were at the next pool. Kelsey, another life guard, looked like she might have been asleep, but maybe she was just paying attention to a specific swimmer. Either way, she'd be no help to Bryan. The mom got out and started to towel off. Bryan admired her ass as she dried her legs. It was decent. A little saggy, but for a woman her age, it looked nicely curved. He lost his train of thought when the kid started screaming again. Bryan slid out of his chair and walked to the dad. "I'm sorry," he said, "but somebody needs to get him."

The dad just stared at his kid. "He's coming." Bryan looked at the mom. She was looking at the kid, too. Bryan chewed on his whistle and looked at the chairs around the pool. Nobody seemed to really be paying attention to the screaming kid. Maybe all the parents were used to screaming, and all the younger people didn't care. One father on the opposite end of the pool was looking at something on the bottom of his foot. Probably a beetle. It was sad to see so many grown ups in faded, old swimsuits, squatting and talking or trying to help their kids put on water wings or sunscreen.

"Listen," said Bryan. The dad leaned towards him and said, "He's coming".

Bryan looked at the breakroom entrance. As he did, he saw Brock Henderson coming in for a swim. Bryan, of course, hated Brock. The pudgy former quarterback who still tried to intimidate people, Brock was a target for a lot of the lifeguards, who'd been on the swim team instead of the football team. Bryan thought Brock's authority should've evaporated at least two years ago. Bryan looked at the kid. He was kind of swimming, but not fast enough. The mom was squatting by the side of the pool and clapping. Bryan noticed the way her suit stretched over her crotch. He wondered if people this couple's age ever went down on each other. It seemed hard to imagine, but some couples their age must've done it. Bryan looked at the diving board and shook his head. The fat kid must've been trying to do a flip, but he just fell face first. It didn't look serious, though. He came up coughing, but swimming and seemingly in control. Bryan heard Brock's voice, "Cryin' Bryan."

Bryan gave a half-hearted wave and tried to very slightly glance at the dad. He seemed to not notice. He was watching his wife watch his kid, it looked like. "Any hot cougars on the prowl?" asked Brock. Bryan mumbled, "Too early in the season." Brock laughed and then spit on the ground. He scratched his gut. If anything about Brock was admirable, it was the fact that he genuinely didn't care what people thought about him, though it's also part of what Bryan hated about him.

The dad yelled, "There you go Skipper." Bryan didn't check to tell if he was really encouraging the kid or if he was just trying to show that he was paying attention. "Look at that fucking kid," said Brock. For the first time all day, Bryan started to actually sweat. If the dad heard, Bryan wasn't exactly sure what he'd do. He hoped some hot girl would walk by to catch Brock's attention. Unfortunately, the next person to come to the pool was a large family with loud kids who had runny noses all the time. Bryan blew his whistle and yelled, "No running" again, to no one in particular. The dad looked at him, then looked around. Brock did an impression of someone watching a cloud. It just made Bryan feel worse. He looked at the diving board, hopeful that someone was doing something dumb. A tall, skinny girl did a nice dive with almost no splash. Bryan wanted to go back in the break room and find Timmy, the lifeguard's mouth-to-mouth practice doll, and beat Brock to death with it. Even in his fantasy, though, Bryan knew that the doll would break without really hurting Brock.

"Look at him," Brock said. "He'll piss in the pool before he makes it to the side."

The dad looked over, and Bryan looked at the diving board. The little girl from before was calling to her mom or dad to watch her. Brock said, "I'd fuck the mom, though."

Bryan wiped at his forehead. The kid was slowing down. The mom was clapping extra hard. The dad was really glaring at Brock now. As much as Bryan hated Brock, he didn't want to watch him get his face beat in, and this dad looked like he could do it. Brock had been athletic, but only had been, and this dad seemed big. On the other side of the pool, a mom was trying to get a little boy to blow his nose. Bryan wondered how young you could be and still have the worst day of your life. "Brock," he said, "pipe down."

"I'd put my pipe down her throat," he said, right away. "Don't cry, Cryin' Bryan. She might still have room up her ass. And that's probably what a fag like you is used to."

Bryan shrugged his shoulders. Brock said, "Imagine her squatting on my cock instead of by the side of the pool." Bryan rubbed at his eyes. Before he had to say anything, he heard the dad. "Imagine my boot knocking out your teeth. Then you'd be able to give a good blowjob to all the old men, you fat fuck."

Brock looked at the dad. Brock seemed surprised. He actually looked at Bryan, and Bryan was very glad for his sunglasses. He mostly watched Brock while he faced the diving board. The dad said, "If you say shit about my family again, this lifeguard isn't going to be able to save you."

Brock looked at the dad, then at Bryan, then back at the diving board. Bryan chewed on his whistle. He felt like blowing it again, just so everyone would look and make Brock feel like even more people would be watching him get dressed down. Brock turned away, "Whatever, Old Man."

He walked off, and the dad watched him go. "Your friend's a real dick," he said. Bryan took his whistle out of his mouth. "He's not my friend. I think he's a dick, too." He glanced towards Brock, who didn't turn back, but who must've heard him.

When Bryan looked back at the dad. The dad was watching his kid instead of Bryan or Brock. "Good choice," he said. Then he walked towards the side of the pool and started clapping. "There you go, Buddy," he yelled. Sure enough, the kid was actually close to the edge. He was breathing hard, but the mom's arms were outstretched. As soon as he was close enough, the mom pulled him in and picked him up to dance with him. Bryan looked back at the parents on the other side. They all seemed to be wrapping their kids up and getting ready to go. Bryan looked over at the other side of the pool. Brock was dangling his feet in the side of the other, smaller pool. Bryan was glad to realize that he didn't feel bad for him. When he looked back at the family, the dad was holding the kid while the mom dried him off. It was a good time to dry a kid off. They'd want dinner soon. They'd go to bed early. And Bryan would be picking up trash and putting lawn chairs away. God knows what Brock would be doing. Bryan wondered how the hell he made money these days. It made Bryan almost believe in a sense of justice, but he watched the fat kid get up again. He tried a flip again, a backflip this time, and just made a huge splash. Some of the other kids laughed. Bryan blew his whistle. They all looked, and then stopped laughing. Bryan didn't say anything, but he felt like it had worked. He looked towards the dad, and he nodded.

A Truly Awful Presence

The summer the demon got into our house was the same summer the last of my baby teeth fell out. I only mention it because I remember how creeped out I was by the possibility of leaving my teeth under my pillow, or anywhere that the demon might steal them. To this day, I don't like my wife to put our son's teeth under his pillow even though I know full well that she and I are the tooth fairy. The demon was a little thing. White and bony with large red eyes and a powerful-looking jaw. We originally thought it was a Beige Fury from looking through Demons of the Third Realm, but it was hard to tell, because all of the pictures were of the demons standing perfectly still. I only ever saw it moving, usually towards me. The demon must've got in through one of our basement windows. We lived in the woods, which isn't really demon country, because it's away from a high-density population, but you're not totally safe anywhere. That's life. Maybe our location saved us from suffering through something even worse.

However the demon ended up in our house, it was an awful thing to have around as a young boy. My parents did their best to shield me, always staying with me and trying to find games to keep me distracted after I finished my homework. But while we were playing Life or Candyland, I'd hear the growling and banging in the basement. My mom would look at my dad, and he'd roll his eyes and go downstairs with a shovel and a stake which, by the end of the demon's run had become as normal to us as a broom or wind chimes. The rest of the game, I'd be clenching my fists and trying not to cry. Dad would come up and say which body part he'd nailed, but the demon always regenerated anyway. Sometimes it would cut off one of its own hands just so that I'd find it, even more claw-like after it sat and shriveled a couple of days. Stuff like this meant that having friends over was out of the question for me, which sucked. I always felt a little embarrassed, and I think my dad was, too.

We'd put up with the damned thing for nearly half a year before my dad broke down and called a professional. It came after my dad made a five-second trip to get me a glass of water before bed. By that point in time, my parents took turns waiting up and sleeping with me. My mom was downstairs with a spray bottle of holy water, a meat tenderizer, and a tall glass of wine (though my parents didn't think I knew). I was finding ways to stall bedtime, so I asked my dad for some water. He looked at me for a few seconds before obliging. The bathroom was just the next door over, so he went and filled up the glass used for brushing my teeth. When we'd go a week or two without it getting close to me, we'd all get careless. The second he walked out the door, that fucking demon came tearing out of the closet and laughing. But not really laughing, not even cackling. It was making a sound that comes from something that doesn't know joy, a sound that comes from something that knows it doesn't understand joy and just wants to mock the very idea.

I started screaming before it got anywhere near the bed, and my dad came running back in. It's one of the few times he actually cursed in front of me. He yelled "You awful shit," and kicked the demon in the face and then beat it on the back of the head as hard as he could. It scrambled away, then crouched and growled. My dad picked up a wooden play sword that a cousin had given me for Christmas the year before, and he swung it at the demon's head. He connected so hard that one of the demon's eyes bulged like it was going to pop. The demon wobbled, fell, then got up again, then fell again. My dad paused, probably surprised himself, and the demon clawed off and crawled out the window. I never looked at my father the same way after that, and I suppose the demon didn't either. It shit on the carpet just before it fell out of my window. My dad look at the shit, looked at me, then yelled my mom's name for her to come up and clean. I didn't say anything, but I knew each parent blamed the other. It was the very next day that my dad sucked it up and called an expert. I felt bad for being the reason he had to break down.

My poor dad, standing there by the kitchen table and watching some other guy talking to my mom about the demon's habits. He stood by me, occasionally tousling my hair, but I could tell he wasn't paying attention to me. Luckily, the demon must've sensed that the guy was there to set things straight. It was very quiet in the house, which usually meant that the demon was setting something up, but you could feel the tension. I looked up to my dad, who was picking at a whisker he must've missed shaving. I leaned against him, and he patted my shoulder. The guy started taking things out of a bag. A gun, a mallet, and a large sword with a gold handle. I leaned forward a little when he took out the sword, as any kid might, and the guy said, "Don't touch it, please."

My father frowned, and I stood behind him. The guy whispered something to the sword, which might've just been for show, as I look back on it now. Whatever it was, I was impressed at the time. We weren't big church goers, so I was always interested in anything that looked like prayer or ceremony. Early in the demon occupation, my mom had gone to the neighbors to ask about demons and angels. The neighbor gave her a book and some herbs, but she never quite figured out what to do. I knew it was a bust, because when my mom returned the book, she gave it back with a single paper plate of oatmeal raisin cookies. I thought about the mason jars of herbs in our basement as the guy kept prepping. They may still be there. I haven't gone into my parents' basement for over a decade, and I still won't let my son look down there, either.

The guy took a candle out of his pocket. It was plain and black. "Want to hold this?" he asked me. I looked up at my dad again, who just shrugged and bent his whisker. I looked back at the guy and shook my head. "He's had some close calls," my dad said. The guy nodded, but I could tell he thought I was being a baby. I really hated him in that moment, which I suppose is what my father felt. I liked that my father and I hated the guy together, and I still like it, as I look back. But it wasn't really the guy's fault. He sheathed the sword, took out a lighter, and lit the candle. It smelled awful. Like the kind of shit you take after two days of hard drinking, but there was also a hint of blood or terror or something. I let go of my dad and covered my mouth. I saw my dad spit on the floor; the only time I ever saw him do that in the house. The stink and smoke kept going for a minute or two, and then the demon came crawling, and I mean literally crawling into the room. It was panting and pawing at the ground. The guy set the candle on the floor, then backed up and grabbed the gun and the sword, unsheathed now. "Stand back," he said. We all obeyed. The demon didn't even look at us, it just crawled towards the candle, drooling as it went.

Before the demon reached the candle, the guy drove the sword through its skull and into the floor. The demon thrashed around, swinging its claws and kicking at the ground. The guy shot at its hands and feet. I'd never heard a gunshot that close up (and indoors) before, and I thought it was deafening. He actually missed more than he hit, and splinters of wood flew up from the floor. But the swinging slowed down. All this happened fairly quickly. The demon was still moving, even as it was clearly dead or dying. Once it mostly stopped, the guy approached it from behind and beat it's head and back with the mallet. The demon split open in lots of places. Gunk oozed and splattered out, and it stunk. I shook a little. The man stayed so calm as he clobbered the thing. I know the demon would've eviscerated me without a second thought, without even a first thought. I know that it was pure evil. But the guy didn't even grunt. Just nothing. I actually felt bad for the demon. And I felt kind of bad for the guy, being able to do that.

Then the guy put his boot on the demon's skull, pulled the sword out, and then swung down on its neck. When the man took his boot off the head, it rolled off and hit the bottom of the kitchen cabinets. The body started smoking, and it turned to ash, though without a real flame. The guy collected the ash in a little vial, then pulled out a bag that he carefully used to contain the head. Thankfully, he cleaned and we huddled, giving a prayer while he did. It may be that this is why I rarely ask my son to pray, particularly not with me. The man loaded the remains up and took them to his truck. When he came back in, my mom was the one to hand him the check. The guy looked at it, then cleared his throat.

"This was actually an Aspardian offender, so if you don't want to pay the full demon rate..."

My dad made a clicking noise with his tongue. He usually gave other guys the benefit of the doubt. He didn't like people looking over his shoulder, so he wouldn't look over theirs, but this was different, it involved my mother. I kind of wanted to see my dad fight the guy. Everything he did with the demon was so prescribed, so ritualized, that I thought maybe my dad could take him if he didn't have his precious tools. I was especially keen on my dad's fighting abilities after the wooden sword. But the guy may still have had a gun on him, and my dad was a fairly laid back, forgiving guy. I don't know if I would've thought it was all that cool to see my dad beat the hell out of someone anyway, if I'd actually seen it up close.

In fact, the only real result of my dad's tongue clicking was for my mom to look at him and then say, "We just appreciate having it gone."

The guy looked at my dad while nodding. "I don't think you'll need me again, but if you do...". Then he looked back at my mom, who looked at the floor, not even replying. "Have a good one," my father said.

The guy left, and my mom gave me a hug. She drove me to the library, then a store, telling me we were going to lay out some circles of protection, get more herbs and do it right. On the ride into town, we really didn't talk, but, on the ride back, she asked, "Do you think we did the right thing?"

I wasn't entirely sure what she meant, so I just said, "Of course." A few minutes later, maybe halfway home I said, "That thing would've killed us. I'm glad to have it gone."

My mom smiled, still looking at the road. "We can have some peace back."

"How much did it cost?"

"Don't worry about it."

"I mean, are we broke now?"

My mom laughed. "You should've asked me at the store. I would've picked up some brownies or something."

I looked out the window. The trees were turning yellow, but only at the edges of their leaves. Mostly, they were still green. "I didn't mean like that. I was just wondering how much the demon set us back."

My mom reached over and rustled my hair. "You don't have to worry about it. We don't have money to burn, but we're doing fine."

I nodded. We were quiet for the rest of the ride home. That night, we laid out the circles, made some bad jokes, and ate snacks instead of dinner. Pizza rolls, which I knew my mom didn't like, but I loved, and I still do. We were quiet, and we giggled. For that night, even when night fell, we were really happy. Things were in that sweet, pleasant realm they went to before they got back to normal. Not that normal was so bad, but it was just normal. Before I went to bed, where I really actually slept that night, my dad took the wooden sword he'd used, and he drew some kind of design on it. It looked like calligraphy, but not any words or even letters I recognized. I looked at him, and he smiled back at me, shrugging. "For protection," he said, "or just to keep busy." I kind of laughed, but I kind of didn't. I still have that sword, or, rather, my son does. Though, to be honest, I don't think I'd know what to do with it if push came to shove. I very much hope it never will.

Man in a Windstorm

This was all at a costume party back towards the early part of my grad school days. One of those grad-student parties where the costumes were more conceptual than actually looking like anything. My costume was a man in a windstorm. I had my hair combed to the side and cemented with mousse, my tie was held out to the side with a coat hanger that I'd undone and slid inside the tie, and I had an umbrella that I'd turned out. Though I'd dropped that almost as soon as I'd got inside. One of the first things that I did, when I got there, was to make a big show of fixing my hair, which remained out to the side. The host let me in, not seeming impressed. I tried to guess what he was. He had on a thrift-store suit jacket with a green mini-skirt with fishnet stockings. "Something with drag?" I asked.

He shook his head and sipped some mixed drink through a crazy straw. It was bright green. "Think stripper."

I nodded. Behind him was someone with a pineapple attached to his crotch. I couldn't tell if the pineapple was real or not. "Something with stages?"

He shrugged. I realized that I didn't know the pineapple guy's name. "Airport-lounge-singer," the host said. I nodded. "Right, I see it now." I think that's when I dropped my umbrella.

"Enter," he said, stepping to the side. I came in and held up my offerings, a half-empty bottle of whiskey and a store-brand version of Dr. Pepper. He smiled. "Nice."

I went into the kitchen area, where this guy with a necklace that had dildos hanging from it was mostly passed out. He was one of those guys who'd been working on his dissertation since I'd started, and I'd never heard anyone seriously discuss him finishing. Other people came in and out, pouring drinks, eating from a bowl of some sort of chips and adding different decorations or bits of vandalism to the dildo guy. I set my bottle aside and poured a little generic gin into a tumbler and tossed some ice cubes in as well. There was a lime out on the counter, and I picked it up and looked for a knife. The lime was the sort of thing that this host would buy to make the drinking better even if everything else was campy. As I scanned the kitchen counter I saw some dirty napkins, a bunch of cigarette butts and a couple of other bits of detritus, but no knife. This guy came in wearing a robe and what looked to be an undone-wire-hanger halo with crude pictures of naked women on it. I recognized him from some of the large grading sessions at the end of semesters, which meant that he must've been an adjunct. He looked at me, "Edward Blitz?"

I shook my head. "Nobody particular, just a guy caught in a windstorm. Are you Caligula or something?"

He shook his head, too. "Sleezus. This is my crown of porns."

I nodded and made what could've been a chuckle. The guy poured some tequila into a jelly jar. Just a little bit. "Nice," I said. "Do you know where a knife is?"

The guy, whose name I remembered as Paul, stuck his hand inside his robe, fished around and pulled out a little jackknife. He opened it and handed it to me. "Thanks," I said. I sliced the lime open and squeezed a little into my drink, then held the lime to him. He waved a hand to decline, then took his hand, then placed the hand on my forehead. "Arise and walk, my son," he said.

I wiped the knife on my pant leg and handed it back to Paul without closing it. "Thanks," I said, again. He took the knife and put it into his jelly jar. Then, he looked over at the guy who was mostly passed out. The dildo-necklace guy. "I could take off one of his ears."

I took a sip of my gin. It wasn't bad for cheap stuff. "Do you know what he is?"

Paul shrugged. "You mean his costume or something else?"

This time I did chuckle. Paul left the kitchen, and I looked at the passed out guy. He must've had about five pounds of dildos around his neck. It made me think that he was riffing on Mr. T, but I wasn't sure. I thought about touching one, but I wasn't sure if this was some piece of performance art to call out anyone who would touch one. It didn't seem likely. He had a pentagram and two phone numbers written on his forehead. I took another sip of my drink and went into the living room, which was dark, but had three disco balls hanging from the ceiling. They were the kind of cheap, lighted things that you buy at Walgreen's. There was also what appeared to be children's art on the walls. It was hard to see what was on there, but it seemed to be a lot of violence and blood on it. I went over to a couple of women who started the same year that I did. Jessica and Alexandra. Jessica was a short brunette, and she was wearing yellow and black stripes with a coat and magnifying glass. I knew that she was studying the rise of detective fiction as a genre, so I pointed to her and said, "Bea Arthur Conan Doyle?".

They both raised their plastic cups to toast my guess. I looked to Alexandra, who had words in lipstick written on both legs. "I can't get yours," I said.

She smiled and put her knees together. "Keep thinking."

I made a show of not being able to drink around my blowing tie. I hadn't drunk gin as an undergrad, though I hadn't drunk a lot of hard liquor. At the time of this party, I was starting to really hit my stride. I couldn't tell what Jessica or Alexandra were drinking. They had red plastic cups. Alexandra was one of those weirdos that seemed to actually get all the theory pretty quickly, so her costume could've been anything. She was wearing a blue dress that was a little short, but I didn't think devil in a blue dress was what she was. I made a dramatic stroke of my chin. "Body of writing?"

She laughed. "That's a good guess, actually. Maybe I'll start telling people that's what it is."

Jessica tipped her cap to me. "What are you focusing on for your project for 781?"

I didn't have a good idea, but part of the game for these sorts of parties was to lie as much as possible, so I said, "I've found this very obscure text that deals with travel and cosmopolitanism from that era."

She nodded. "Who's your theorist?"

I looked out at the room. There was a man with an arrow through his head and a plastic fish sticking out of his suit jacket. I recognized him as Steve Martin, though he was missing the glasses with the plastic nose. "I don't even remember his name," I said. "Something that starts with an 'M'. But he wrote a lot of letters about dietary customs."

Alexandra hiked her skirt up a bit. Her panties had a target drawn by the crotch. "Get it?" she asked.

I tried to look unaffected. Alexandra wasn't beautiful, but she had a directness that could overpower me. It pointed out to me my general lack of finesse when it came to women. "The dark continent?" I asked.

Alexandra and Jessica both laughed. Alexandra touched my arm and then walked off. Jessica leaned in. "I didn't catch what she is, either."

That actually did make me feel better. I pointed to a wall. "Do you think he's hung onto that children's art from the time he was a kid?" I asked her.

She looked. Near us, there was a drawing of a figure with what looked to be a bright green wound on his head. I tried to remember if Vulcans had blue blood or green. I thought blue, but I could've been wrong. "No," she said. "I think he had his students do these in class one day."

I looked at another one nearby. It was of a passable spider eating what looked to be a tank. "No shit?"

She took a sip of her drink. "He told them that it was about understanding primitivism, crayon and children's images, so that they could better understand the limitations and inspirations of low modernism."

"How does he get away with it?"

Jessica smiled at me. "Balls." It was the kind of thing that

Alexandra would've said. I was surprised to hear Jessica say it, but I smiled and drank. There was a sort of dance circle starting in the room. They had some lounge version of what I think was an Iron Maiden song going. I couldn't place either the song's name or the performer. Some asshole was doing John Travolta's half of the Pulp Fiction dance right in the middle of everyone.

"Yeah," I said, "I heard he has three testicles."

She laughed, and it occurred to me that I might be hitting on her. I knew this would only get worse as I continued drinking, but Jessica wasn't a bad woman to hit on. A bit insecure, but short and fairly pretty, she was the kind of woman who might actually have sex with me out of boredom, and she was fun to talk to. Alexandra was fun at a party, but I couldn't imagine talking to her one on one.

The Steve Martin had gone behind the Travolta dancer (who was dressed as what I thought to be Barbara Bush), and was making faces and adjusting his crotch. If it had been later in the night, there might've been a shoving match. Instead, the Travolta dancer turned around when he saw that people were laughing. He saw the Steve Martin guy who froze and gave an exaggerated smile. The dancer punched him in the arm and then went to a corner of the room and sat on the floor. The Steve Martin guy pretended to faint. Feigned a faint. I looked at his cup, a little dribbled out, but he must not have had much drink in it. I wondered how long it took to clean up after parties like this.

I looked at Jessica. She tucked a stray hair behind her ear. "Do you know what you're taking next semester?"

I wondered if Alexandra had left us alone to make us flirt, making us like captive animals in the zoo. The class talk made me feel depressed. I said, "Speed," and took a large drink, trying to look flatly earnest.

She nodded. She was right, it wasn't a great joke. "You?" I asked.

Jessica shook her head, "No thanks."

Steve Martin got up crawled along the floor into the kitchen. He left his cup on the floor. I was going to ask her about Ten Little Indians, which I'd heard was actually good, but a large group came into the party. They were younger than I was, and they were very rowdy, which was a good sign. I saw a cousin of mine among them. I'd known that she was going to school in town, but we never made a point of seeing each other anywhere. Before I could stop myself, I said, "It's my cousin."

Jessica looked. "Someone dressed up as your cousin?" she asked.

I suppose that I should've told her that she was being stupid, but I was so surprised that I couldn't respond in any meaningful way. My cousin was wearing a trenchcoat, a grey number that looked to be from a thrift store, though it's possible that it was her father's. My uncle had been any number of things before settling into retail. A trenchcoat would've suited him. But she didn't wear it for long. After saying hello to a couple of people, my cousin dropped it to the floor without particular care. She was stark naked.

"Seems nice," Jessica said.

I nodded. "Nudity runs strong in my family." I drank more, trying to erase any sense of awkwardness or propriety. It seemed weird that someone whom I'd seen play Barbies would be walking around naked in a room of my colleagues. I supposed most of them were someone's younger sibling or cousin.

I watched my cousin, as many of the partygoers did. She looked young to me, though I'd ogled students of mine who were her age. "What's her name?" Jessica asked.

"Ann," I said. It seemed like I should've added something, but I wasn't sure what. She wasn't my most rebellious cousin, but I wasn't surprised that she was naked, either. In fact, I was more surprised to see her at the party at all. Vanilla Ice came on the stereo. It was the metal version of "Ice, Ice Baby". A one-hit wonder covering his own song. I wondered if my cousin knew what it was.

She saw me and came over. "Hey", she said, seemingly as surprised to see me as I was to see her. I felt like I should feel bad for not having contacted her earlier, but maybe I would've seemed creepy to her.

"Hey," I said. "I'm a man caught in a windstorm."

She nodded. "I'm a nudist."

"I see that." Then, to Jessica, "This is my cousin. Ann."

Jessica nodded. "You look ready for a good time."

"Is this your girlfriend?" Ann asked.

I laughed, my typical sign of both success and defeat. Jessica said, "That Blanche Devereaux is a real slut."

Ann looked at me. "Does it feel weird to see your cousin naked?"

I shook my head. Behind her, I could see a couple of guys, composition guys, both of them, nodding and watching her. "No," I said. "Remember when your older sister was younger? She used to run around naked all the time." The guys pulled over another guy, a lit guy who I think was specializing in the Restoration period. He raised his eyebrows, but didn't react beyond that. "But she'd squeal and run away if you told her she was naked."

"Like Adam and Eve," Ann said. Jessica laughed, and I looked around the room. I felt like I was probably supposed to want to protect Ann, though I realized that she'd probably been having sex for at least a year or two by now. Maybe more. There wasn't much to do in small towns like the one she grew up in.

"Well," Ann said, looking at Jessica. "Have a good time."

"Likewise," I said. My cousin wandered off, not directly to the composition guys who had been ogling her, but I figured that that stop wasn't far off. One of them had nailed at least a dozen of his students. He was one of the darlings of the program, of course. Jessica said, "Nice gene pool."

I looked down at her. "Were you going to take a dip?"

Jessica smiled and touched my chest. "You are a dip."

I touched my glass against her red plastic cup. "Have a good time," she said and went back to the kitchen. I drank my drink. The gin tasted warm. Or tepid, maybe. I wandered around the room, nodding to people and looking at the artwork. There was a good one of two dogs eating a space ship. I saw Jessica come back in and go to talk to some baristas that the host was friends with. Probably angling for a joint. My cousin was twirling her hair around one finger and talking to the people she came in with. One of my colleagues was wearing doctor scrubs with fake blood and holding a plastic baby doll with a coat hanger stuck through the doll's head. In his defense, he'd fashioned a hole in the doll's head to hold a shot glass, so it was functional. I saw Alex go to my cousin. They giggled a bit, then kissed. I couldn't tell if it was lust or performance art, and that made me feel bad, too.

I went to the kitchen. This time, I mixed myself a Dr. Pepper knock off and whiskey. I looked at the dildo guy. By now, he was definitely passed out. I thought about how I actually could cut his ear off, though I didn't have Paul's knife anymore. I decided to pick up one of the pens on the counter and draw a keyhole on one of the open spots on his forehead. I had it most of the way done when a young couple came in. The guy had a Nixon mask that was resting on the top of his head, and he was wearing a bra with pasties on it. The girl was just in jeans and a flannel shirt. Her story must've been amazing. Or terrible. "What's that?" the guy asked.

"A keyhole," I told them.

The girl nodded. "Nice," she said. "Like Alice in Wonderland."

I laughed. "Exactly. Right."

I finished the keyhole, then finished my drink. I was still giggling a little, though not out of happiness or humor. The reference made me think of the accusations against Lewis Carroll. Another example of a childhood memory defiled. I couldn't remember his real name. Dodgson, I think. The couple poured their drinks and went back in to dance. I decided to take a coffee mug out of the host's cabinets and pour my drink into it. I'd take it home with me. The neighborhood was bad in the way that there would be people asking you for cigarettes on the way home, not in that you'd be getting mugged. If somebody asked me, then I'd give them the drink. Give it to them in this guy's mug, then walk the rest of the way home and drink alone. If nobody asked me, then I'd drink as I went home, jerk off while thinking about Jessica, and go to sleep. I'd give the host back the mug at a later party, when I needed an opening line. It was the kind of thing that the host would appreciate. Which I guess made me a good guest. But it's not something I could've planned. Taking the mug. It's just where I got taken.

Feeling Not So Hot

'm pretty close to done with the oranges I'll have to peel. They're the little oranges, the clementines, so peeling them can be a pain, and it doesn't help that Dad's telling us a story about how oranges used to be this huge prize, "delicacy", he says in Europe centuries ago. Like he's a citrus expert. It's because they didn't have sugar like we do, is what he says, and chocolate tasted like cocoa instead of like a Nestle's Crunch bar. And I'm not even thinking about chocolate. All I'm thinking about is how my dad just doesn't get that hearing that people used to have to wipe their asses with leaves or filter their water through something weird doesn't make Frankie or me appreciate things. It's like telling us that kids are starving in Rwanda. It's not like we send our uneaten food there, so if I toss out something gross, like that nasty Salisbury steak, then it doesn't change that there are starving kids, so what does that help? I think he just wants us to talk about Rwanda in front of other people so that they all think his kids are really informed or something.

Dad tells Frankie, "We're lucky," and Frankie just coughs really loudly. I'd like to think that he's sticking it to Dad, but he's too young to think like that. Frankie still thinks Dad is awesome, which I guess is okay for a little boy, but he'll figure it out eventually. Still,

Dad can't yell at Frankie, but he's totally lost his steam in talking about ancient Europe and the great history of selling chocolate. So I peel open another orange and watch Frankie, who's been turning the same orange around in his hand for about five minutes now, like there's a pull tab or something. Bobby Munson said that the Japanese are trying to genetically engineer apples that have stems you can pull that'll actually slice open the peel, but Bobby Munson has to go to this special counselor, I hear, so I never believe most of what he says, which Mom told me was a good policy after I'd told her some of the things that Bobby Munson says.

We hear Mom coughing from her room off and on, where she's watching TV in bed. She doesn't watch that much, but when she's sick, she likes to just sit there and zone out. Sometimes you'll go and ask her what she's watching and she'll look at you and say, "What?" The weird thing is that she watches really dumb stuff. I know that she's smart or whatever, but she watches stuff that even I think is dumb, though I guess if she's not watching it, maybe she wants it to be really dumb. Or maybe it's smart and I just don't get it, like that "world poetry" book that my mom told me to read. It was like they took the most interesting or big stuff and talked about it in the most boring way half the time so that English teachers and social studies teachers could yell at their students for not caring enough, which Mr. Wilson does so much that everybody in school does an impression of him yelling. Jenny Wagner's is the best, because she has the hand gestures down perfectly. Though I did like the one poem about the tree that all those people were climbing and sitting in. It reminded me of The Giving Tree, even though that book really bummed me out, even as a kid, because the tree ends up this total stump and the man's all old and probably will die soon, and then the tree's just a stump because of some dead guy.

I'm trying to remember some of the books that I really liked as kid while Dad's started in again, this time talking about sailors and scurvy, and Frankie keeps interrupting him to ask about Captain Jack Sparrow and it's kind of funny to see Dad keep trying to stay on task, but I can't laugh or they'll both get mad, so I just keep trying to remember all the books I liked as a kid. I get some of the Dr. Seuss books mixed up. How do you tell if the guy was playing a trombubler or a crogtrapulator? And if he was doing it to help the Lorax or to fight about butter? You can kind of imagine this one big Seussworld where they all have their own countries, like the Grinch might go to Catmerica on vacation or whatever, and everybody behaves in the same weird and stupid way, which I guess is kind of like high school. Especially the pep rallies. But it always seemed funny when my mom read those books to me. But half the time what you really liked as a kid is really stupid when you look at it again. Like Strawberry Shortcake or something. It makes you wonder why my parents let me watch it, but I guess most kids' stuff is at least kind of dumb, although maybe that's an "important life lesson", like Dad would say.

My dad tells us that we can take a break and "enjoy a segment". Sometimes he sounds like a newscaster or gameshow host or something. It's weird to say "enjoy", especially because this is supposed to be to make us feel better and not even to taste that good. I wonder what's in my dad's head when he enjoys something. I could almost see him thinking, "I enjoy this" when he's eating an orange or reading a book like a book of poetry that Mom gave him to read and that he reads to "broaden his horizons" which wouldn't be the only reason that Mom gave it to him. I wonder if he was always this way. Mom doesn't really tell us much about what he was like before they were together, but I wonder if he was always kind of a robot. I mean, yeah, he's a nice robot like the one from Centennial Man, but is that what I'm going to end up marrying? It seems like he could've been romantic before Frankie and me, but it's really hard to see what that would've been like when he's lecturing us on cocoa and scurvy and stuff. Not that I'm that interested in my dad's life before our family, I guess. It's funny, though, to think about some dude in college peeling oranges and thinking he's really smart for beating a cold. "How's yours?" he asks me.

I hate these kinds of things, because it's not like he's being mean, but I just don't feel like answering. And then I feel bad because I shouldn't give him trouble about this, either, but sometimes I just want to hole up in my room like Mom, but Dad gets this way when Mom gets sick. Like he's a babysitter, like I'm going to run into her room and bother her if he doesn't keep me busy. Whatever.

I shrug and nod, which is like Frankie's cough where he can't really react one way or the other, so he asks Frankie, and Frankie says, "Yeah," and I'm not sure if Frankie's even listening. Sometimes he's weird. I mean, kids are always weird, but Frankie zones out in a different way than Mom and the TV. He zones out like he's looking for ghosts or something that nobody else sees. Maybe he thinks robots are going to fly through the window or something, and maybe that's how Mom and Dad met. Maybe he flew through the window when she was sick and he was a robot with a basket full of peeled clementines, and maybe she sits in her room waiting for a newer, better robot each time she gets sick, and now I feel like laughing, but if I do my dad'll never let me wave it off.

But I wonder if Mom sees being sick as a break from us all. My parents had a talk, at some point, with us about how we're a traditional family, but they're not necessarily traditional parents. I still don't know what all that was about. I mean, I get it: Mom works but she feels like she should do a lot with us, but Dad wants to do his share, too, so we should think of them both as people we can talk to about all things. But, come on, I'm not going to go talk to Dad about dating or something. Not that I talk that much with Mom, but Dad would, like, sit me down and make "pro" and "con" lists and develop a plan for who I'm going to ask out and "on what timetable", but Mom at least knows that sometimes I just want her to tell me that I'm right to hate this one girl. Like Carly Stevens. It's not like she ever did anything that bad to me, but she's just always there and always cutting on me, and I should just shrug it off, and I usually do, because my friends all think she's a bitch, too, but Dad would try to figure out which teacher I should talk to and explain to me how to "best represent my perspective" or something, something that he'd say in a business meeting, but Mom at least knows that a lot of life is kind of crappy, and that's all there is to it one way or the other, I guess. And that definitely makes me sad, but she doesn't try to fix it, because I guess she knows the world can't really be fixed, and trying to figure out these stupid plans is just pretending that things can be figured out. But it doesn't make a difference except to make you feel "empowered", but you know that's just a guidance-counselor word, so what's the point? It's like arguing about which computer is better. You might be right, but you're not going to change any of the dorks' minds, so why even think about it that much? But people are always worrying about the stupid little things, I guess.

And then I hear my mom laugh. Maybe Ellen's show is on? I realize, then, that I don't even know what time it is, and it's possible that Mom's laughing at something that's not even on the TV. Maybe her robot hero did come and told a really funny joke while handing her the first clementine segment. Dad sweeps up a big pile of peels and dumps them in the trash. I smell my fingers and it's not really good or bad. It smells like the ghost of oranges or something. I guess it could be worse. Maybe that's what these oranges are like. They're like the parents I have that aren't bad, they want me to be good and they do do stuff for me, but sometimes you just wish they'd be drunks or gone a lot so that you could have some fun. But you can't turn that kind of thing off or on, and either way it probably seems like it sucks half the time. Or more, if you've got the drunk kind, probably.

But that's not really like oranges. I guess that when you spend a long time peeling these stupid oranges, that's how you start to think, and so everything seems like oranges to you. Though maybe the oranges really are like my little brother, sitting there and playing with the last of the peels instead of either helping or even eating the stupid little segments. Maybe these oranges are a lot of trouble and they still could be bad and you have to take in a lot of them to feel better at all, and even then, you don't know if it was the oranges that really helped make you better or if the virus or whatever you had just died. But I guess that means that I'm not that great either, which I basically know, but it feels kind of crappy, looking at Frankie and thinking it. That's like life, though. Or that's what I'm supposed to deal with so that I can be an adult, because that's something we're all supposed to want to be for some reason. We're all supposed to be some cold-stricken lady hiding away in her room while her family is stuck peeling the little oranges her husband buys to keep the kids occupied so she can stay in her room laughing and coughing at God knows what awful program is on the TV or other thing that's going through her head. And I'm thinking about that, and I look at Dad, and he looks surprised that I'm making eye contact, so, while I have him surprised, I ask, "Can I be excused? I want to lay down in my room."

And I see him doing some kind of math problem in his head about what the right answer is, or maybe he's about to tell me that I should've said "lie" instead of "lay" or something, but then he actually smiles at me and says, "Sure, Honey," and turns to Frankie so that they can compare hands after peeling the oranges. And I get up and say, "Thanks," really quietly, because it's the only way he'll know that I'm saying it for real. And when I get to my room, I really do lay down or lie down or whatever, and I close my eyes and I breathe in. There's a little bit of orange smell, but that's okay for right now, because I can just relax and be sick, which is what I'm supposed to be today, I guess. In a couple of days I'll be better, and then I'll have some other problem, but for now I can just enjoy my bed and not feeling so hot like my mom.

Part of Our House

There's a man who lives in our house. I think it's a man. It doesn't seem like something a woman would do, although I guess I don't know. I mean, I've never seen whoever it is. But my dad always says "he" or "him" when something happens. The last piece of cake or pie will be gone, and Dad'll say, "He ate it, didn't he?" and my mom'll say, "Rick", which is my dad's name. I guess she thinks that things could be worse. That creeps me out, because it makes me wonder what he could do. This guy. Like, could he kill us? Or what if he tried to have sex with me in the middle of the night? Probably he wouldn't do either of those. Or, if my parents thought that he might, I hope they'd move us. Though maybe he'd move with us. I don't know where exactly he stays. Either way, I wonder if he watches me when I change or shower. That's really, really bad.

But probably he doesn't, because it seems like there's things that he will do and things that he won't. Like if company's coming over, then nothing big happens for a few days before they come. No company food gets eaten, just leftovers and things like that, and things stay pretty quiet so that my dad doesn't go off about things. It's kind of nice when company comes, I guess. When it's just us for a long stretch, sometimes weird things come. Nothing really bad, but more like the time that Mom brought me home from school and in the kitchen he'd stacked a bunch of canned vegetables in this tall column. She didn't say anything, and I was young enough that I guess I thought fairies or elves or someone did it. I remember her sending me to watch cartoons, so I was happy, because usually I had to do homework right after school.

Then there was the day when he left one ham sandwich in each room of the house. Mom noticed that the bread was gone, so she went to the store, and I found one in the living room. A ham sandwich. Then I found one in the bathroom, he'd put it by the spray. Then I checked my room, and he'd put it under my dresser. I went in to Mom and Dad's room, which I hardly ever do, and I opened Mom's dresser drawer. It was with the socks. I threw them all out, and I swear he must've watched me do it. I was sitting by the picture window, just kind of curled up on the couch when Mom got back from the store. I think she knew what was wrong, and maybe she talked to whoever it is, because it never happened again. Still.

I don't remember a time where little things didn't happen, so maybe he's always been here, since I was a baby. What if he stood over me while I slept in my crib? How old was he then? It's a lot to think about. It makes me wonder if that's part of why Mom and Dad didn't have any more kids. Like they thought that they could have a kid in the same house as this guy, but then Dad got too creeped out by having his little girl in the same house as this guy, and so he wouldn't have any more. Dad seems to know what he does and what he doesn't do. The time I broke that California plate from our trip a few years ago, I tried blaming the guy, but Dad just punished me for breaking it and then gave me extra punishment for lying. It sucked.

But they had me, and they didn't give me away to keep me safe, which I'm glad for. And maybe he's not really a creep, maybe he's just a decent guy who's too spooky to be out in the world. Like Boo Radley. Not bad, just always in a corner. And if I told the other girls at school, maybe they'd tell me he was probably someone famous gone into hiding or a prince that saved some kids from a burning building, but his face melted, so now he can't go out in public. But if he was really a good famous person or a prince or something, then wouldn't he leave me flowers and not ham sandwiches? So he must be like Boo Radley, so I wouldn't want to marry him, because then you'd have a husband who doesn't work or talk to you, he just hides in the corner or basement or something. Maybe the garage is where he stays. And even if he is a prince, is that something you'd really want to live with? Even if he is a hero, would you really kiss Boo Radley?

Convergence

A sequence is defined as a function (not a "series of numbers," because that would confuse later definitions) with a first number, a second number, and so forth for all the integers from one to infinity. Another way of putting it is that an infinite sequence of numbers is a function whose domain is the set of integers greater than or equal to some integer n_0. Some of these sequences will converge, and some will diverge. Convergence means that each successive term gets closer and closer to some number. Divergence means that the sequence never settles on a single number.

***

We were both in the classroom early. Calculus II, even though this was my first semester. There were one or two of our classmates there, but most of the seats were open, so I sat in Laura's general vicinity. She was looking at the textbook and tapping her lips. When I sat down, she briefly looked over at me and gave a fraction of a smile.

"What do you think of this class?" I said.

She looked over at me. "It's all right so far, I guess. Little early to tell."

"Mhm. The professor can be a little long winded."

There was a slight downturn in Laura's lips after I said this. "I think he's all right. I don't know any of the profs, but one of my friends who goes here recommended him to me, actually."

I nodded and began to study my own textbook. If she didn't know any profs, then, she might well be a freshman like myself, and this could indicate that she would be single, again, like myself. If she did not want to be attached when heading off to college, it would be likely she'd be available at this early point in the semester.

***

A series is the sum of the terms of a sequence. So, if you add up all the terms in a sequence, you have a series. Even if a sequence converges, its corresponding series can still diverge. A sequence converging is a necessary condition, but not sufficient one for proving a series converges. Take, for instance, a sequence where every term is one. Clearly, that sequence converges to one. However, if you add up an infinite number of ones, you will go off to infinity. Your sum will be amorphous and inconceivable to the human mind.

***

Through our study group (something encouraged by our TA), Laura and I got to see a fair amount of each other. A typical session might go something like this:

Laura: Number 23 converges.

Group member #2: Converges, or converges absolutely?

Me: Just converges. Use the comparison test, then the integral test. (Various mutterings of other group members.)

Me: (To Laura) What did you end up doing last weekend?

207

Laura: I just stayed in and watched a movie with my roommates.

Me: Nobody wanted to go out?

Laura: One of my roommate's friends called, but I didn't feel like going out with him. I think she's trying to set us up.

Me: But you're not interested.

Group member #1: Compare it to one over root 2n?

Laura: Root 3n. Root 2n would actually be less. You want to show it converges.

Group member #1: Oh. right.

Me: But you're not interested?

Laura: No, I'm not too into him. Did you do anything exciting?

Me: No.

***

If a series has no negative terms, one can use the comparison test to prove whether the series converges or diverges. The comparison test involves, first, a conjecture; if one assumes the series converges, then one finds a larger sequence known to converge, proving that the series in question, being smaller, must converge. Conversely, if one assumes the series in question diverges, then one finds a smaller sequence known to diverge. Thus, although one will not find the actual sum of a given series, one at least can determine whether or not a finite sum exists. Sometimes, this is the best for which one can hope.

***

After one of the group sessions, I walked Laura to the bus stop. There was an elderly man waiting for the bus. He sat silently and didn't look directly at us. She and I were discussing a future session. "Maybe this weekend we could get together and look it over?" I asked.

She bit her lower lip. "I don't know. I kind of like my weekends to be weekends, you know?"

I looked down.

"That doesn't necessarily mean that you and I can't do anything this weekend. Just maybe not math."

This response was in excess of my expectations. "That sounds great."

I took her hands and gave a slight squeeze. We smiled at each other, there in the dim light of the bus stop, and we even kissed. Imagine what the old man must have thought. What he told his friends about us.

I asked her if she wanted me to wait with her for the bus, but she said she'd be fine, and that I should go. I already had her phone number for study-group purposes (easy to remember, the last four digits were a Pythagorean triple given the proper placement of commas), so we kissed once more, and I was off, though I kept a half eye on her until the bus came, given the old man.

***

You can express the concept of convergence graphically with a line and a number of points. The points may get closer and closer to the line from above, from below, or alternating. They may poke above and below the line, never quite touching, but always getting closer. Always approaching that stable mark. You might think of the points as straddling that line. Or jumping over it. Becoming more and more standard while still moving.

****

Let me try to describe her. Laura has blonde hair; she also has green eyes, nice, high cheek bones, and a trim figure. Not emaciated, but slender. The only real abnormality of her physical appearance is a tiny discoloration on the side of her left nostril. Most people who see it mistake it for a small stud in the side of her nose, but it's actually a birthmark. It's barely noticeable. In fact, as we spent more time together, it became just a general feature to me. Something there, but almost imperceptible. In fact, things progressed quite well. At the end of the semester, we'd even agreed to meet for New Year's.

****

Although you can't add together infinite numbers of numbers, you can, at least, approximate the sum. Sometimes this is done by integration, which is really an artificial infinite sum, if you think about it. It employs mathematical formulae and equivalences to come to some kind of expression, which gives the sum. The theoretical number arrived at is, oddly enough, more accurate than any summation which could be done by hand.

****

I wanted to wait until I was out of my parents' house to do this (for obvious reasons), so, as I was leaving town to meet Laura, I stopped at a gas station. I deliberately picked a fairly small station that would require a key to the bathroom so that I could have some privacy.

I went inside and obtained the key from the clerk, a bored looking man who referred to me as "Pal."

210

The bathroom was not heated, and not very well lit, but beggars can't be choosers. I brought out the nub of a carrot I had in my back pocket, a cigarette lighter, and the needle. I then tore a bit of paper towel off the dispenser over the sink and set my tools on the paper, as the sink did not look particularly sterile. Rubbing my hands together for warmth, I took a few deep breaths. When I felt ready, I picked up the lighter and needle and held the needle over the flame, to sterilize it. I then set them both back down onto the paper towel. I slid the nub of the carrot up my nose, which proved to be very uncomfortable. The needle was still a bit hot to handle effectively at that point, so I stood, looking in the mirror and trying not to sneeze. I had to sniffle enough to stop the sneeze, but not so much that the nub would wedge itself too high up my nose. I tried holding the nub and sniffling, but this was neither more effective nor more comfortable than sniffling without holding it.

Before long, my eyes began to water, and I decided that I would have to go ahead with it before I was unable to function. The acceptable margin of error was slim. The needle was hot, but not unbearable. The pain as I pushed it through my nose was not as terrible as I feared it might be, but it bled a bit more than I expected it to. I pulled the needle back and forth in the hole to try widening it a bit. I let the wound bleed into the paper towel as I took the tiny bottle of rubbing alcohol out of my jacket pocket and folded up another piece of paper towel to soak up the alcohol. As I removed the first paper towel, I saw a representation of Laura's birthmark, slightly expanded from where it had bled out.

The pain of the contact with alcohol, especially on the rough, gas-station, paper towel, was worse than the original puncture. I dabbed and wiped until it seemed to be mostly done bleeding. I threw away the needle and carrot nub, stuffed the alcohol and lighter into my jacket pockets, and went back to the gas station attendant.

Bill, as his nametag indicated, still looked bored, and either didn't notice or didn't comment upon my new feature. I did leave the bloodied paper towel on the bathroom sink, though, so I suspect he had some excitement later in his day as he tried to formulate a narrative of what must have gone on in the bathroom. Bloody paper towels, a needle (if he could find it), and a carrot nub. What would it add up to for Bill?

***

Different types of series and sequences will converge more quickly than others. For instance, the multiplicative inverse of the iteration's number N_i squared will converge, but not nearly as quickly as a geometric series will. Some series will converge at a logarithmic (slow) pace, whereas others will converge at an exponential (fast) pace. The pace of convergence is clearer further on in the series (when n is large) than it is early on (when n is 1, 2, etc.).

***

Laura and I sat down on the hotel bed. "So," she said, "tell me how Christmas with your family was."

I told her that it had been a generally enjoyable trip, and she then told me that her Christmas had gone fairly well. Apparently a relative had flown in from somewhere to be with the family. I think it was an aunt from Maine, but I could be wrong. I was having difficulty focusing.

It wasn't until that night that she said anything about my nose. We were lying in bed, laughing over the fact that she'd told her parents we were using separate hotel rooms (her parents tended not to be as progressive as mine), when she pulled me closer to kiss me. After the kiss, she looked at my face and asked, "What's that?"

I smiled. "I poked myself."

She bent her head back and rolled her eyes. "Well obviously. How did you do it?"

I put my arms around her and pulled her closer. "With a needle. I heated a needle and pierced my nose."

Her body went rigid in my arm. "Why would you do that?"

I quickly explained to her my decision to approximate her. "It's bringing the two of us closer together," I said. "The process of closing in on you physically brings me towards you on a number of levels."

***

A series that converges due to its terms alternating between negative and positive converges conditionally, but it may not converge absolutely. A series converges absolutely (is absolutely convergent) if and only if the corresponding series defined by the sum of the absolute value of each term converges. Converging absolutely is stronger than converging conditionally.

***

Her hand went up to her mouth and she looked away. I waited to see if that moment would bring about a union or a division. I cannot possibly convey to you the terror I felt at that moment.

213

Much like with love and physical pain, the most intense moment with terror is that moment of anticipation. I saw a tear run down her cheek, which only confirmed my suspicions.

"Laura," I said. "It's because I love you."

She turned to me, touched my cheek with the same hand that had just been to her face, and said, "It's beautiful."

I wrapped my arms around her and kissed her. "Beautiful, like you."

She began asking me about the particulars of the operation. How long I'd been planning it, how much it hurt when I had done it. The pain got exaggerated a bit, as I described things. I told her about the gas station attendant, and we laughed. As we exchanged kisses, we created different scenarios together from the details I shared with her.

Laura: Were you rubbing your nose when you went back in?

Me: I imagine so. Why?

Laura: I bet he thought you were a coke fiend. You had some kind of mishap in the bathroom.

Me: I'm on my last legs.

Laura: You've been snorting it for years, and your septum is gone.

Me: It's destroyed my career and torn apart my family.

Laura: You were heading South, trying to outrun your debt.

Me: Even in the cold, I was sweating like mad.

Laura: Just paying your bill you were about to crack.

At this point, Laura reached over and put her hand on my cheek so that her thumb touched the scab on the side of my nose. "You know," she said, "now that you've run away from your wife and kids, there's no turning back."

I reached over to touch her face so that my thumb touched her birthmark. "There's only one thing left for a desperate man to do."

Laura smiled at me. She took her hand off my face and slid it down to my chest, then to my belly. I won't go into the sordid details. I'll merely say that the two of us coupled and then stayed up to watch the ball drop at precisely midnight.

The Posted Limit

The father drums his fingers on the steering wheel. It had been the best day. The one that they'd all remember as they tried to look past the bad ones. The father knew he'd been going a little fast, feeling invincible and maybe wanting to enjoy that. Now, he looks at the day as the prick cop takes his time getting out of the car. The lights are flashing and all these other cars are whizzing by at indeterminate speeds. There's a blue sports car with flames on the side. It seems like that's the car that should be pulled over. The father worries that he has ruined his son's perfect day. This day, his son's smile was a full step beyond angelic. Angelic has always struck the father as vague. Blonde and without real emotion. His son, bald from treatment, gave a smile that was precious for both its weakness and its rarity. It was something given to him and his wife because they were already stretched so thin in finances and energy.

The cop car's door was opening. He wasn't fat, really, but the father could see that it took him two or three tries before he could get himself out of the car. The father would like to curse, to let out a string of vile obscenities, but he was already too deep in karmic debt. He assumes, watching the cop walk, that this is not the type of guy to let him off with a warning. The father looks at his son in the rearview mirror. He will not turn around, at the moment. The son is 13 years old. He should be starting to scream at his father, telling him that he doesn't get it. Telling his friends that his father is lame. Instead, they're too often silent together, having too much of weight to discuss and too little of levity to laugh about.

The cop reaches the window, and the father rolls it down. This is the third time he's been pulled over in all of his life. It's been a long time. He has one of those awful moments where he knows exactly what's going to happen before it comes. "Do you know why I pulled you over?" The cop asks. It's a quiz where every answer is wrong. "I guess I was going too fast," the father says. How to balance humility and strength. "You know how fast you were going?" the cop asks.

The father hates this man. "To be honest," he says, "I sort of lost track."

There's little reaction from the cop. "I clocked you at 73. Do you know what the posted limit is?"

Given the place that he was pulled over, the speed limit could be 65 or 55. The father tries to guess not what the correct response, but the appropriate response is. "I thought it was 65," says the father. He's heard that a cop won't pull you over if you're going seven miles or less over the speed limit, but he can't place where he would've heard that information.

"Can I see your license, registration, and proof of insurance, please?" The father assumes that his answer was correct, or he would've been corrected. As the father reaches back for his wallet, he wishes his son's cancer upon the cop. He wishes the vomit, the waiting around in hospitals and the despair all upon this man. He pulls at his wallet, but it catches on his pocket, having angled as he pulls. On the road, a black minivan goes past at what seems an incredible speed. The father is beginning to sweat.

After getting the wallet out, he has to flip through a number of receipts and very few bills to find his license. He sets the wallet in the passenger seat, empty so that his wife can sit in the back with their child. His wife has said nothing this whole time. He can't meet her eyes. Next, the man opens his glovebox, moves aside a map and a flashlight to find his insurance card. Below it is the owner's manual. He looks at it to make sure that it's the most recent one before handing that and his license to the cop. The cop takes it and heads back to his car.

With the cop back in his car, the father rolls up his window. He looks at his son. "Sorry," says the father. The son shrugs. "73 isn't that big of a deal."

In this moment, the father loves his child. He quickly looks to the mother, who shrugs. A kind noncomittment. "It is speeding," says the father, turning back towards the windshield. The son says, "Yeah, but people are passing you by."

The father checks his rearview mirror again. The cop is still in his car. "Tell him where we were," says the son. The father thinks about this. If he tells his son that it doesn't matter where they were, it cuts his son's day. If he tells him that it does, then he's drawing from his son's illness. This event, this thing with the cop is throwing off what they'd banked on learning about justice and power in the universe. The father looks at his wife's eyes in the rearview mirror, but he cannot interpret her face. He considers this, too, but before he can say anything more, he sees that the cop is almost back at his window. He pushes the button to make the window go down.

The cop leans against the frame of his car's window. "There a reason why you were going so fast today?"

The father shrugs. How could he communicate this day to the cop? How many days before would he have to include? The cop nods to the father's shrug. He must've seen this before. As the father resigns himself to a ticket, the son speaks. "Sir," he says, "there is a reason why my father was going so fast."

The cop peeks into the car. The father watches his face tighten as he really sees the son for the first time. A sickly, hairless boy slumped against his mother. He has to see the basics, the facts of the situation. But the father stares ahead, looking out the windshield. He sees the daylight just beginning to wane.

"Today," the son says, "I got a wish granted. Or, I got told that I would get it granted. You might even see it on the news tonight."

The cop runs a hand over his mouth.

"I have cancer," says the son. "My dad just wanted to get home to celebrate."

The father watched the cars go by. Which one has the wealthy, asshole teen trying to impress his girlfriend? Which one has an alcoholic on his way to a bar? "You have cancer?"

"Terminal," he says back.

The cop must feel trapped, locked in. In a different world, the father would laugh. "Terminal," the cop mutters. His saying it eats away at something, but it doesn't kill it.

"Yep," says the son. His voice is flat but strong. Maybe this still is about power.

The cop turns his face towards the father again. "I'll let you off with a warning, but take it easy, all right?"

The father turns his face towards the cop slightly, but not his eyes. "Thank you officer," he says.

The cop turns back to the son. "I'm sorry," he says, and the father hates him again. His pleasant politeness showing that this world is alien to him. The father doesn't register his son's response, but he expects that it's kind and wisely noncommittal. The cop seems satisfied, anyway.

The father waits for the cop to get back in his car and drive off. He leaves the window open, feeling the cool air coming in. As the cop drives by, the father holds up a hand, a gesture that the cop will read as good will. Which is fine.

After the father rolls up his window, the son says, "What a prick." The father doesn't think it worth the time to pretend to correct his son. Today is precious. He isn't wrong, either. "I agree," the father says, making eye contact in the rearview mirror. The mother sighs. "You boys," she says. This works like a joke, and the father and son smile. The father starts the car, signals and gets back on the road. The family heads for home, carrying with them a different story than the cop has.

Fomite

A fomite is a medium capable of transmitting infectious organisms from one individual to another.

"The activity of art is based on the capacity of people to be infected by the feelings of others." Tolstoy, *What Is Art?*

Writing a review on Amazon, Good Reads, Shelfari, Library Thing or other social media sites for readers will help the progress of independent publishing. To submit a review, go to the book page on any of the sites and follow the links for reviews. Books from independent presses rely on reader to reader communications.

For more information or to order any of our books, visit
http://www.fomitepress.com/FOMITE/Our_Books.html

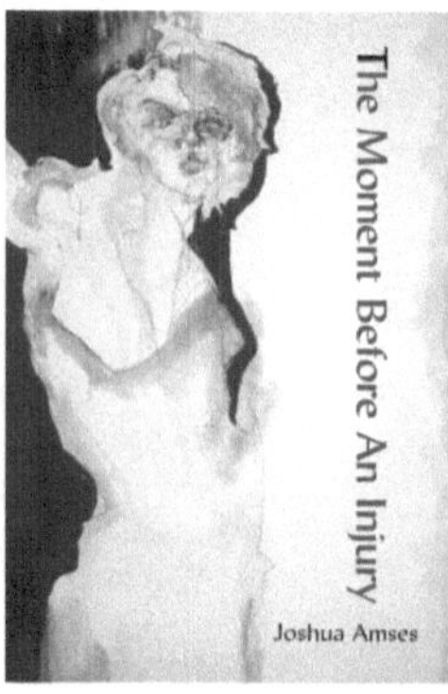

Nothing Beside Remains
Jaysinh Birjépatil

*The Way None
of This Happened*
Mike Breiner

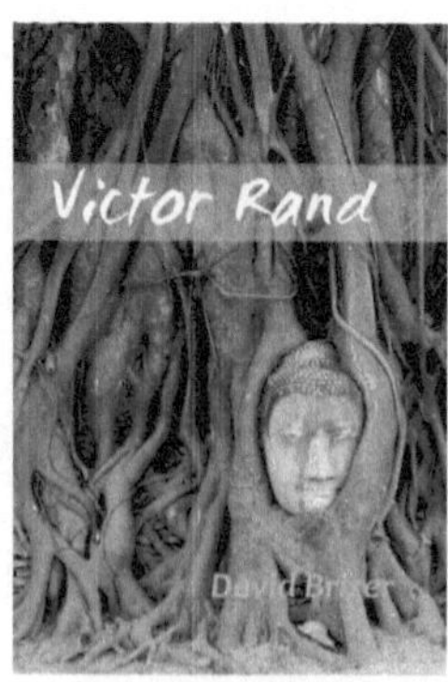

Victor Rand
David Brizeri

Cycling in Plato's Cave
David Cavanagh

Picking Up the Bodies
James F. Connolly

Fomite

Unfinished Stories of Girls
Catherine Zobal Dent

Drawing on Life
Mason Drukman

*Foreign Tales of
Exemplum and Woe*
J. C. Ellefson

Free Fall/Caída libre
Tina Escaja

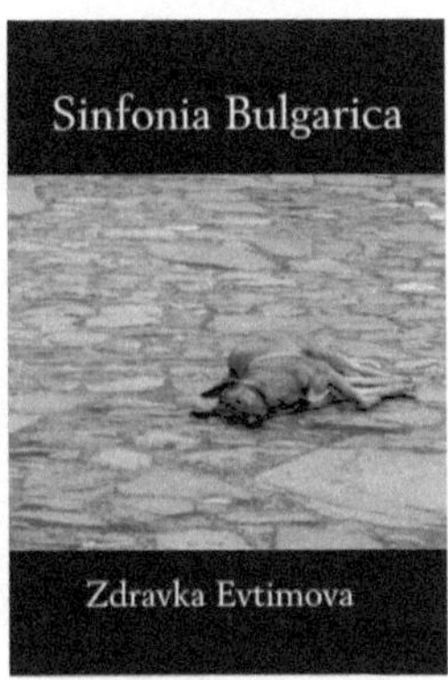

Sinfonia Bulgarica
Zdravka Evtimova

Derail Thie Train Wreck
Daniel Forbes

*Where There Are Two or
More*
Elizabeth Genovise

*The Hundred Yard
Dash Man*
Barry Goldensohn

*When You Remeber
Deir Yassin*
R. L. Green

Fomite

*A Guide
to the Western Slopes*
Roger Lebovitz

Confessions of a Carnivore
Diane Lefer

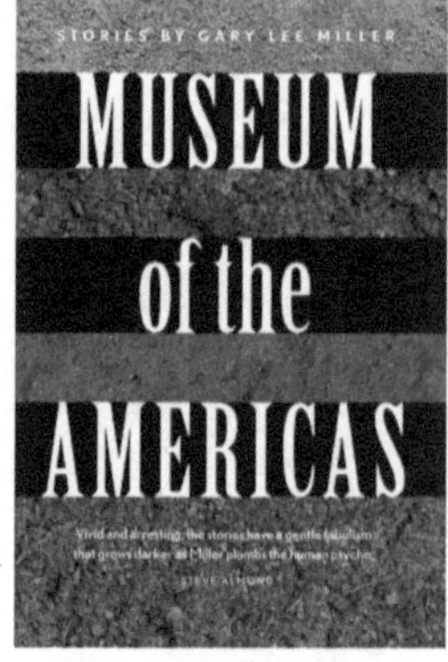

Museum of the Americas
Gary Lee Miller

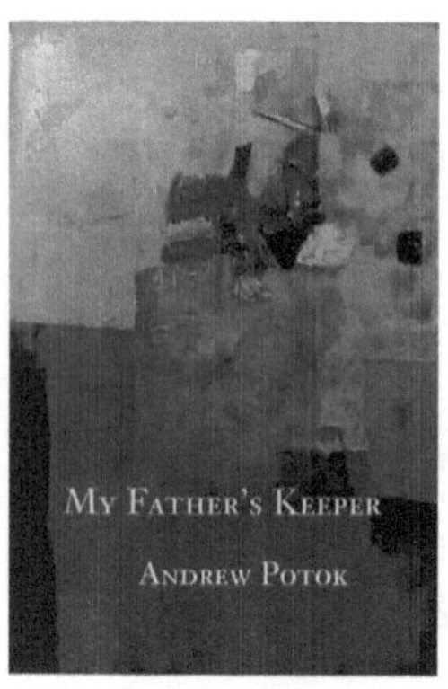

My Father's Keeper
Andrew Potok

*The Hole That Runs
Through Utopia*
Joseph D. Reich

Companion Plants
Kathryn Roberts

Rafi's World
Fred Russell

*My Murder
and Other Local News*
David Schein

Bread & Sentences
Peter Schumann

Fomite

Principles of Navigation
Lynn Sloan

Among Angelic Orders
Susan Thoma

Everyone Lives Here
Sharon Webster

The Falkland Quartet
Tony Whedon

*The Return of
Jason Green*
Suzi Wizowaty

*The Inconveniece
of the Wings*
Silas Dent Zobal

More Titles from Fomite...

Joshua Amses — *Raven or Crow*

Joshua Amses — *The Moment Before an Injury*

Jaysinh Birjepatil — *The Good Muslim of Jackson Heights*

Antonello Borra — *Alfabestiario*

Antonello Borra — *AlphaBetaBestiario*

Jay Boyer — *Flight*

Dan Chodorkoff — *Loisada*

Michael Cocchiarale — *Still Time*

Greg Delanty — *Loosestrife*

Zdravka Evtimova — *Carts and Other Stories*

Anna Faktorovich — *Improvisational Arguments*

Derek Furr — *Suite for Three Voices*

Stephen Goldberg — *Screwed*

Barry Goldensohn — *The Listener Aspires to the Condition of Music*

Greg Guma — *Dons of Time*

Andrei Guruianu — *Body of Work*

Ron Jacobs — *The Co-Conspirator's Tale*

Ron Jacobs — *Short Order Frame Up*

Ron Jacobs — *All the Sinners Saints*

Kate MaGill — *Roadworthy Creature, Roadworthy Craft*

Ilan Mochari — *Zinsky the Obscure*

Jennifer Moses — *Visiting Hours*

Sherry Olson — *Four-Way Stop*

Janice Miller Potter — *Meanwell*

Jack Pulaski — *Love's Labours*

Charles Rafferty — *Saturday Night at Magellan's*

Fomite

Joseph D. Reich — *The Derivation of Cowboys & Indians*

Joseph D. Reich — *The Housing Market*

Fred Russell — *Rafi's World*

Peter Schumann — *Planet Kasper, Volume 1*

L. E. Smith — *The Consequence of Gesture*

L. E. Smith — *Travers' Inferno*

L. E. Smith — *Views Cost Extra*

Susan Thomas — *The Empty Notebook Interrogates Itself*

Tom Walker — *Signed Confessions*

Susan V. Weiss — *My God, What Have We Done?*

Peter Mathiessen Wheelwright — *As It Is On Earth*

www.ingramcontent.com/pod-product-compliance
Lightning Source LLC
Chambersburg PA
CBHW061432210726
48287CB00007B/2184